Enjoy)
and
enjoy To

David Entwistle
2007

Thomas the Adventurer

Kingly Boredom

David Entwistle

Bloomington, IN   Milton Keynes, UK

AuthorHouse™
1663 Liberty Drive, Suite 200
Bloomington, IN 47403
www.authorhouse.com
Phone: 1-800-839-8640

AuthorHouse™ *UK Ltd.*
500 Avebury Boulevard
Central Milton Keynes, MK9 2BE
www.authorhouse.co.uk
Phone: 08001974150

This book is a work of fiction. People, places, events, and situations are the product of the author's imagination. Any resemblance to actual persons, living or dead, or historical events, is purely coincidental.

First published by AuthorHouse 11/9/2006

ISBN: 1-4259-3685-7 (sc)

Printed in the United States of America
Bloomington, Indiana

This book is printed on acid-free paper.

Cover design by **James Lord (www.chewstudio.com)**

To my Nephew Jude

Thomas the Adventurer in

Kingly Boredom

1st Chapter
Royal Trouble

Once upon a time, there lived a small German king called Thomas. He was very, very, very, very bored and always looking for something to do, but to no avail. Everything had already been done.

One very sunny day, Queen Esmerelda sat upon her throne doing her knitting. There beside her, on an equally golden throne, sat her husband, King Thomas. He was, as usual, quite bored. The Queen leant over to the King,

"Do something!" she snapped.

"What?" protested the King.

"Anything--anything will do, as long as I don't have to keep listening to the shuffling of your feet and the tap, tap, tap of your fingers on that throne."

Thomas paced the Throne Room floor as he tried to think of something to do.

"Stop pacing!" yelled the Queen. "It's annoying me!"

Thomas threw his hands up in despair, "I'm trying to think of something to do."

"Well—jolly well think somewhere else!"

The King gave a deep sigh; "OK, ok--I'll go outside."

The King ventured out into the Rose Garden and as he did an idea hit him; "I know what I'll do! I'll pick some roses for Esmerelda to cheer her up. After all, there are plenty out here and she was rather upset with me."

Thomas started picking. He picked and picked and picked and just when he thought he'd run out of roses he found some more, so he picked them too. "That should be enough," he thought and made his way out of the very empty-looking garden.

The King entered the Royal Throne Room holding the roses behind him. As he did, the Queen gave him a glare; "I thought you were going to do something?"

"I did."

Esmerelda's eyes narrowed with suspicion; "What did you do?"

Thomas showed her the flowers he'd been hiding behind his back; "I picked you some beautiful roses," he smiled.

"Oh how very thoughtful of you. Where did you get them from?" asked Esmerelda, cheerfully.

"Oh just outside," Thomas shrugged.

Suddenly, the Queen's mood changed to one of panic and horror, "Outside! Not my Rose Garden?" she cried.

Thomas was rather cautious, "Erm...yes. Is that a problem my dear?" he asked.

The Queen seemed to calm down for a moment; "A problem? No, it's not a problem."

Thomas sighed with relief, but as he did, Esmerelda screamed, "It's a horrible catastrophe--a disaster in every way! I spent ages taking tender care over that garden, watering every rose individually, and even talking gently to each one to help it grow. Then **you**," she pointed at the King, "in a matter of minutes, destroyed it all. I bet there's not one single rose left on one single bush!"

Thomas gulped; "I'm so sorry; please forgive me my dear. I just didn't think." He paused for a moment; "Will you forgive me Esmerelda?"

"Give me a day, maybe a week," snapped the Queen.

King Thomas ventured back outside into the beautiful sunshine and sat down upon the drawbridge to his castle. He sat down to think, and think he did; "What can I do now? I can't do anything indoors, because it's boring, but then again there's not much to do out here either."

Suddenly, an idea struck the King like a huge bolt of lightning; "That's it!" he said, jumping to his feet. "I know what I'll do. I'll go and find an old friend. Surely they'll be able to help relieve me of my boredom."

The King paused for a moment to think of someone to visit; "I haven't seen Manual for a while. I wonder how he's doing these days?"

Manual the Know it All lived in the Poo Poo tree in the small village of Lapoopascoopa, in the region of Latwoilet. It was about a five to ten minute walk from the castle, so the King thought he'd take the Royal carriage and save his very precious energy.

When the King arrived at Manual's tree house he knocked on the thick oak door; it caved in. "That's a little strange," thought Thomas, as he peered into a rather dark and empty tree. "It seems as if he's moved without letting me know. Oh well, never mind. I'll just ask one of the locals if they know where Manual lives now."

The King approached a strange looking little man with no hair. A huge boil took up most of his head and his lips were well hidden behind a long, scraggly, white beard.

"I'll just ask this strange little fellow if he knows. Excuse me, my good friend, do you know where Manual the Know It All has moved to?" asked Thomas.

The old man shifted suspiciously; "Firstly, I'm not your good friend, and, erm," he thought for a moment, "oh yes, he lives four trees down on Burloak Avenue."

"Oh thanks very much."

"You're not thinking of paying him a visit are you?" asked the old man, with some concern.

"Yes, why?"

The strange old man rolled his eyes, "Oh nothing, nothing," he said and continued on his way.

Thomas arrived at Manual's tree and knocked three times.

"Oh come right in, it's open. Just leave any weapons and unlawful habits outside." The voice of Manual the Know it All was strangely squeaky and sounded very educated.

Manual sat Thomas down on a colourful couch with a colourful cup of tea.

"How's the King these days?"

"The King is very bored," complained Thomas.

"Oh well, it's a good job you came 'round to see me today. Yesterday, I finished my amazingly interesting handbook to boredom. It's called: 'Boredom-a Simple Solution."

The King was not impressed, "Oh...erm--I'd rather just do something else."

"Nonsense. You must listen to my amazing revelations. They will help you my good man."

"Oh, ok, but only a small part," pleaded the king.

"Of course, of course," replied a rather unconvincing Manual.

Manual the Know it All placed his red stool next to his red bookcase and reached up towards his newly finished red book.

"Ah, here it is. You'll love it," said a rather overexcited Manual. "Now, let us start our journey to recovery in Chapter 1, as it is at the beginning and so easy to locate."

"Oh boy," Thomas sighed.

"Paragraph 4 of Chapter 1 illustrates how herbal teas can help release the chemicals in the brain that help fight against boredom and boring thoughts. One scientist from Brooglestien illustrated this for the scientific community last Sunday at the convention for..."

By this time in the monologue, King Thomas had fallen asleep and Manual had not even noticed. So absorbed was he in his own amazing revelations that he couldn't even hear the King's incredibly loud snoring. The same incredibly loud snoring that would keep Queen Esmerelda tossing and turning all night long.

King Thomas began to dream. He dreamt he was on the Planet Boredom where all the little green men were even more bored than he was. The little green taxi drivers were too bored to drive the same old routes. The little green people were too bored with their jobs to work and there was no TV as the little green viewers were too easily bored with all the shows.

"This is terrible!" thought Thomas, as a little green person fell asleep right in front of him. It was at this point that he awoke.

Thomas woke up to find that Manual had got to Chapter 2, paragraph 9, of his guide to boredom and it was a quarter past the hour of four.

"Tea, sir?"

The King swung 'round to see who had spoken; there stood a very aloof looking man holding a tray of tea and biscuits. It was Manual's butler. The tea and biscuits did seem rather tempting, but all the King wanted to do was escape; "No tea for me, thank you. Look, I've got to go now. If Manual should ask after me, tell him I had an important engagement to go to," Thomas paused, "a year long one."

"I understand **completely**, sir."

2nd Chapter
On the Path to Excitement

Amazed and exhausted, the King stumbled out of the tree and into quietness; "Ah, that's better. How can anyone talk that much? He never used to be like that, well not since his dog Agrobar ran away."

King Thomas thought aloud as he walked along the Forest path, "How can I shake off this boredom? I wonder if I have any exciting friends?"

Suddenly a high-pitched voice squeaked, "What about Nico the Excitable?"

"Who said that?" asked the King as he scanned the forest.

"I'm up here."

"Where?"

"In the tree right in front of you, second branch to the right."

Thomas looked up. Finally, after a little while, his eyes rested on a small white figure perched on a little branch; "Oh yes, I see you. You're an owl."

The owl rolled his eyes, "How very observant of you."

The King looked rather puzzled; "Owls don't talk."

"Yeah I know, that's what my mum said," replied the owl.

"What's your name?" asked Thomas.

"Ollie."

"Aha, Ollie the owl. How very original," groaned the King.

"Well, I like to think so. Anyway, I recommend Nico the Excitable to you because looking at your face I can see you're in need of some, pretty desperately."

Thomas hung his head; "Yeah, you can say that again."

"Well, I like to think so. Anyway, I recommend Nico the Excitable to you because looking at your face I can see…"

"You've already said that!" interrupted the King.

"I know. I have a good memory. You said, 'Yeah you can say that again,' so I did."

"Oh gosh Ollie," complained Thomas, "that wasn't what I meant."

"Well, you must say what you mean."

"You're nuts!" snapped the King.

"Oh no thanks, I've just eaten."

Thomas groaned and made a motion to leave, "Well, I think I'll be going now before you drive me mad."

"I'd like to drive you to mad, but I don't have a car."

"Just one more thing Ollie."

"Yes?"

"Where does Nico actually live?"

"Oh yes, I'm ever so sorry, I forgot to mention that. Nico lives in a rather large clearing, in a rather large tent, in the rather large Forest of Excitement. It is north from here, down Las Vegas Fairview, opposite the Post Office. It's about fifteen minutes walk and roughly seven minutes and thirty-three and a half seconds from our present standing. You can't miss it, it's a huge white tent."

"Ok, thanks Ollie."

"No problem," said Ollie as he looked backwards to make sure Thomas was going in the right direction, and flew straight into a tree.

After thirty-two minutes of walking towards the Forest of Excitement the King thought to himself, "How would Ollie know how long this walk takes? He's an owl, he flies."

As the King paused to rest a moment, he saw a funny-looking man in a funny-looking clown suit staring at him in a funny-looking way.

"I say good chap, could you help me straighten my nose?" The voice was rather jolly and it belonged to...

"Are you Nico the Excitable?"

"That's what all my modestly well-behaved friends call me."

Thomas stared at Nico's orange curly hair, huge boots with bells on and ridiculous oversized clown costume and bluntly said, "You look like a freak."

"Thanks very much; that's the nicest thing anybody's said to me all day. You can come over to my tent for tea."

The King looked terribly confused, "Excuse me, but I just insulted you."

"Oh, don't worry about that old boy, happens all the time."

"But doesn't that bother you?" asked the King in surprise.

"No, I'm used to it," said Nico. "Sometimes my passion and excitement get the better of me and off I go getting people wound up again. Freak is the tamest of words I've had launched at me today--besides which, it's all rather exciting, don't you think?"

The King was still rather baffled by this odd man with his odd ways, but gave a polite nod anyway.

Suddenly, Nico looked at his giant clown watch and froze with excitement; "Tea's at six and it's 5:59 right now, which is rather exciting because it means we have sixty seconds to get home or my wife will leave me."

Thomas was amazed; "Your wife would leave you for being late for tea?"

"Yes, it's an exciting motivational threat. She won't **really** leave me, but I motivate myself through exciting challenges and you never know, she might just carry it out."

"What would you do if she did?" asked Thomas.

"I'd be bored, because my wife..." Nico paused and his face went bright red, "Well, she is rather exciting."

"Oh, I see."

Nico and the King arrived at the 'Tent of Enthralling Excitement' (or Nico's place for short) at **6:05** and walked through the giant tent flaps.

As soon as Nico appeared in the lounge, he was greeted by his wife, Nadi; "Nico, you're late again," she said.

"I know honey-bunch, but isn't it all so exciting?" replied Nico, as he collapsed into his favourite chair.

Nadi frowned, "Er..no, it's not."

Nico was cautious; "Are you gonna leave me?"

"Yes," replied Nadi, firmly.

His face suddenly changed, "What!"

"Yeah, I'm gonna leave you," she kissed him on the cheek, "in about eighty years."

Nico breathed a sigh of relief and asked an exciting question: "Anyone for some wine?"

"Er, yes that'll be nice," said the King.

Nico walked up to his wife as she sliced vegetables in the kitchen. She turned to him and smiled, then whispered, "Who's your fat friend?"

"He's not really fat, and I'm not sure he's my friend yet, and his name I do not know."

Nico walked out of the kitchen and back into the lounge, where the king patiently sat. He turned to Thomas and asked, "What's your name Bob?"

"Er no, it's Thomas; **King** Thomas."

Nico was shocked; "**King** Thomas?" Wow! I didn't know you were a **king**!"

"Well, neither did I 'til my dad died."

Nadi poked her head around the kitchen door and looked at her husband, sternly; "May I speak with you for a moment, Nico dearest?"

"Of course, sweetie."

Nico merrily entered the kitchen. Nadi slammed the door behind him.

"Yes dear?" said Nico, rather innocently.

Nadi burst open with frustration, "You brought a **king** here to our house?"

"Yeah, I mean I didn't realise he was a king."

Nadi was furious, "Nico, our house is a mess, our garden is a mess and I have no food here...no food fit for a king, that is!"

"Oh isn't it all so exciting?" replied her husband, with great gusto.

"Any more of that and you're sleeping on the couch," snapped Nadi.

Nico threw his arms up in protest; "Well, what can I do about it, he's here now?"

"Politely and enthusiastically get rid of him," replied Nadi, through gritted teeth.

"But my dear, he's our guest. I can't just chuck him out."

Nadi gave her husband the most awful glare, "Would you like **me** to do it for you?"

"No, I'm the man of the house. I will do it, and besides," he smiled, "it might be exciting."

Nadi sighed; "Is there **anything** you won't do for excitement, Nico?"

"I hope not my dear, I hope not."

Nico walked out of the kitchen and back into the lounge where Thomas was looking even more bored than ever. He placed his glass of wine on the table next to him and, with a touch of irritation in his voice, asked Nico if everything was alright

"Er, no actually," replied Nico hesitantly, "you have to leave. I'm ever so sorry; it's my wife you see. She's not ready to entertain a King. I should have asked her before inviting you over."

Thomas' stress and frustration began to boil over, "Well, where can I go now?" he moaned, "I thought you might be able to cure my boredom by giving me some exciting things to do."

"I'd love to old man, but I'm afraid tonight's just not a good time to help you," Nico thought for a moment, "however, I do have a friend who's always helpful to me when I'm unsure what to do next."

"Who's that and how long will it take me to get to him?" asked, a greatly irritated, Thomas.

"My good friend, Bob the Unusually Wise, should be able to help you. He only lives about five minutes down the road in the Castle of Enlightenment."

"Unusually wise, ay? Sounds good to me," replied Thomas, as got up to leave; "Well, I'll be going then."

"Ok, so sorry about all of this old chap. It's just one of those things. Perhaps you could come over next Wednesday?"

A voice came from the kitchen, "No Nico, we have the mayor coming for dinner Wednesday."

"Oh yes, thank you Nadi dear, I almost forgot. How exciting!" Nico turned to face the King, "I guess you're going to Bob's then?" he asked.

"Er, yeah I am," replied, a rather demoralized, Thomas.

"Oh, how exciting!"

"Well, I'm glad to be out of that mad place," thought Thomas as he walked down the road and away from Nico's tent.

3rd Chapter
A cure for Boredom

After a while, Thomas turned a corner on the forest path and suddenly caught sight of a huge fortress. It towered above the trees.

Finally, as it was beginning to get dark, the King arrived at Bob's castle. He crossed the drawbridge, said "hi" to the two guards on duty, and pushed the unusually large doorbell. Soon afterwards he heard the chiming of many bells and the door creaked open to reveal a man of rather small stature.

"Hi, my name is Bob the Unusually Wise. What can I do you for?"

Thomas gave a deep sigh, "I'm bored."

Bob peered at the King through the darkness, "Yes, I can see that, but what do you want me to do about it?"

"I want you to help me."

"It'll cost you," warned Bob.

"Money, you mean?"

"Yep, definitely."

The King was rather suspicious, "I have money, but I don't know whether you're any good yet."

Bob was very persuasive, "Oh, you can pay after therapy."

"Oh good," replied Thomas, his spirit starting to lift a little.

"Shall we start then?" inquired Bob.

"Are we gonna do this indoors?" asked Thomas.

"It'll cost you more."

"Oh that's ridiculous," moaned the King, "it's cold and dark out here."

"Yes I can see that. I am unusually wise, you know."

Thomas gave a deep sigh of frustration; "Oh brother. Ok, let's just get on with it."

"Inside then?" suggested Bob.

The King lost his patience, "For Pete's sake, yes!"

Bob and the King ventured into the castle and closed the door behind them. It was as black as coal. You could not see a jolly thing.

"It's dark in here," said Thomas.

"Yes, I try to conserve energy, it's very wise you know."

Bob and Thomas fumbled around in the darkness until they found a large elevator to take them to the top floor of the, obviously modernized, castle. Once the elevator reached its destination, the doors slid open and they stepped out into another dark room.

"I can't see anything," moaned Thomas.

"That's 'cause it's dark," replied Bob.

The King rolled his eyes in disbelief; "Yes I can see that, but can you hit the lights?"

Bob looked confused; "I don't see how hitting them will help."

"Are you sure you're wise?"

"Yes, unusually so."

"Then use your amazing wisdom and switch on the lights in this room, so we can at least see what we're doing."

"Ok, ok, no need to get impatient," complained Bob.

Bob flicked the light switch. The room was a mess-- books everywhere, stains in abundance. The place looked like it hadn't been swept in years.

Thomas was amazed, "This place is a mess, doesn't that bother you?"

"Oh no, it's wise to have a bit of clutter. I always like things I need to be in the last place I left them. If I put anything in a drawer or cupboard I'll forget I have it. Anyway, enough chit chat, what can I help you with?"

The King could not believe his ears. Was Bob asking him what was wrong all over again? Thomas almost collapsed under the weight of sheer frustration; "I'd like to be cured of boredom," he replied.

"Wouldn't we all?" laughed Bob, "but it's not that easy. I believe if you really want to be cured it's going to take a lot of guts and bravery."

"I don't care. I just want to be cured," snapped Thomas.

"Ok, I'll tell you how, if you just sit over there on my black leather couch."

"How can you afford a black leather couch?" asked the King, in amazement.

"I've got a castle, haven't I? Besides, all professionals have a black leather couch."

"I suppose you're right," moaned Thomas.

"Of course I'm right, I'm always right."

The King sneered, "Love your humility."

"Me too," agreed Bob.

Thomas and Bob waited, awkwardly staring at each other.

"What are you waiting for?" asked the king.

"I'm waiting for you to sit down."

Thomas was growing very hot under his kingly collar; "Why didn't you just tell me to sit down?"

"I thought you would have been wise enough to have concluded that if you were to get any therapy from me you would need to sit down on the black couch," explained Bob in a matter of fact way.

"Well, it's polite to ask if someone would like to take a seat. After all, I'm not a mind reader, am I?" moaned the King.

"You can't take a seat from my house," said Bob, as he rather protectively clutched his black leather couch.

"I didn't mean it like that," fumed Thomas, "does nobody understand me today?"

Bob put his arm around the King, "There, there old
bean. No need to get a bee in your bonnet over this. We'll
have a bit of therapy and it'll all be sorted out, ok? I mean,
I'm not just anybody, I'm Bob the Unusually Wise."

Thomas gave a deep sigh; "So, can I sit on the couch
now?"

Bob smiled, "Of course you can."

King Thomas lay down on the black leather couch.
Bob pulled up a wooden chair and began to speak ever
so gently, "Now just relax, that's it, just close your eyes.
Imagine you're on a beach. The waves are lapping against
the sandy shore. A servant is fanning you, while another
massages your feet. The sound of my voice is a gentle
breeze, a whisper of the wind."

Bob continued to speak very quietly, while king
Thomas dozed off.

Three hours later Bob shook the King, "Your session's
over."

"What? I've been asleep. Surely **that** doesn't count as
therapy."

"Oh, it most certainly does," replied Bob.

The King was shocked, "How could me falling asleep
have been therapy?"

"Well, you weren't bored were you?"

"No, I suppose not," replied Thomas as he rubbed his
eyes, "but I could have slept at home.

"Yes, that is true," agreed Bob, "but not quite as peacefully." He thought for a moment, "Out of sheer interest, do you have a family? If I had a family, I'd never be bored."

Thomas looked confused, "What do you mean?"

"Well, I'd play with the kids, go for romantic outings with my wife. I certainly wouldn't think of myself, 'cause that's boring."

The King leapt to his feet, "That's it! You're a genius Bob!"

"No, I'm just unusually wise."

"I'm so bored because I've only been thinking about myself and my own needs. If I thought of others more than myself, I would find excitement every day."

"Well, of course," shrugged Bob.

The King made ready to leave; "I'll be going now."

"Not without paying, you won't!" replied Bob with outstretched hands.

King Thomas thrust a vast amount of coinage into Bob's hands.

Bob was shocked; "Wow, that's a lot!"

"You're worth it!" smiled the King as he headed for the door.

Thomas skipped out of Bob's place, thumbed a ride and made it back to his castle, only to find all the lights out. It was late and his family were all asleep.

The King entered the castle. He went into his son David's room. Thomas had forgotten how very valuable

23

his son was to him. A tear fell from his cheek and touched the edge of David's face, "Sorry I haven't always been there for you son," he whispered.

Then he ventured into his daughter's room. Lucy was very much in dreamland. He stroked her long blonde locks and leant over her. He gave her a kiss on the cheek and whispered, "Goodnight my princess; tomorrow we'll play."

Then he climbed the stairs to the upper chamber where his beautiful wife lay. The King gazed at her for a few moments then slipped into bed. He whispered, "I love you. I'm sorry I haven't always been around. I've only thought of myself, and that's boring. I'm gonna be around more now, I promise."

"Good, 'cause I missed you," whispered Esmerelda.

Thomas gulped, "I thought you were asleep."

"No, I'd only just gone to bed."

"About earlier, I'm..."

The Queen interrupted him; "No, don't." She put her finger over his mouth, "that's boring!"

The End.

King Thomas the Adventurer in.....

Run Lucy Run

Chapter 1

Convincing Lucy

One morning, King Thomas took a stroll near his castle. Suddenly, someone sped right past him. He'd never seen anyone walk that quickly. The walker was a little blonde haired girl in a pretty pink dress, fastened with a pretty pink bow. Her hair had been tied into pigtails and they swayed from side to side as she disappeared into the distance. By the time Thomas recovered from his surprise enough to call out to her it was too late, she was gone.

After his stroll, the King entered his castle. He spotted his wife, Esmerelda, in the distance. She was busy painting a picture. As Thomas entered the room she smiled and said good morning, but he walked right past her and slumped down into a chair.

"Well it **was** a good morning," moaned Thomas, "until I got overtaken by a sweet little child on my morning walk."

"Really?" asked the Queen, in surprise. "Well there are some fast young lads around today, so I wouldn't be too upset."

"It wasn't a young lad; it was a young lady."

"Oh dear," said Esmerelda, trying not to laugh.

Thomas was far from impressed; "It's not funny dear, a man in my position overtaken by a little girl, it's highly embarrassing!"

Esmerelda pretended to be serious for a moment, "Yes, your position was certainly compromised," she paused trying to keep her composure, "I mean you didn't exactly finish in pole position." The Queen held her sides to stop them from literally splitting with laughter.

"Well, I knew **you'd** understand," said Thomas, sarcastically.

After she had regained her composure Esmerelda said, "So what was this dear little wonder-walker like?"

"She had long blonde hair and a pink dress on."

The Queen suddenly became quite interested and stopped the painting she had been so busy with. She walked over to her husband; "Was her hair in pigtails?" she asked.

"Yes, indeed it was."

"Oh, I know who that was. You were passed by Judy Finnimore, fastest girl in all the Kingdom."

Thomas sat up in surprise, "Really? How did you know that?"

"Oh I know her mother Dana, we often meet at various school and social activities throughout the year. You've nothing to be ashamed of, Judy's often proved difficult to catch and almost impossible to beat.

"But that's ridiculous, she's just a child."

"Yes and you're just thirty or so years older my dear, that's quite a difference. She's actually competing this Saturday at the Regional Junior Athletics Championships. Dana invited me to go along with the kids and watch. You're very welcome to come."

"It's so unfair Esmerelda," sulked Thomas; "Why are only females allowed to participate in athletic activity?"

"Honey, you were the one who changed the law. The old law did not allow females to do anything athletic and **forced** men to try out for various athletic tournaments. Then you became King and decided that it would be way too strenuous for you to do any athletics, but not wanting to lose the entertainment of it all you wrote a new law. This law, which cannot be revoked by even the King himself, allows only females to do athletics. I can run to my heart's content and you can laze around all day, just like you always love to."

"Oh yes, I'd forgotten that very sexist law of mine, but I was in a bad mood when I wrote it. Isn't there a bad-mood-get-out clause?" moaned the King.

"I'm afraid not my dear, but you can always come and watch, if you like."

Thomas was adamant, "No, I'm going to participate. They will make an exception for the king."

"They might," smiled Esmerelda, "but do you really want to race against a bunch of little girls?"

"Well, actually that would seem just a trifle daft," laughed Thomas.

"I have a better idea. Why don't you encourage Lucy to join in this year?"

Lucy was the King and Queen's daughter. She had never been interested in athletics and felt that being the slowest girl in her class was a good enough excuse not to even try to compete in any championships.

"You'd have more success teaching a polar bear to tap dance sweetheart."

"That's not kind; probably true I guess, but not kind. You're always avoiding her and putting her down when she doesn't meet your grandiose expectations. Perhaps it's time to cut her some kingly slack and give her a chance?" suggested the Queen.

"Alright, but even if I can get her to agree, I know as much about athletic coaching as a camel knows about deep sea fishing."

Thomas knocked a few times on his daughter's bedroom door. As she opened up Lucy was surprised to see her father standing there. Rarely was such a visit made. Frantic thoughts started to buzz around her head; "She wasn't in trouble was she? Something had happened to mum, hadn't it? It wasn't her bedtime already, was it?"

Just as she was about to think another frantic thought her father spoke, "I'm sorry to interrupt you honey. Were you doing your homework?"

Lucy sighed; "No homework in the summer holidays, dad."

"Oh no...I suppose not. No wonder there's so many kids running around like headless chickens, causing daily heart attacks for their worried parents."

"Yeah, but not for you. No offence dad, 'cause I know you're the king and all that, but you couldn't care less what we do. The only time you get that worried is when you've missed an opportunity to complain."

"That's not true!" protested Thomas. "I do worry about you, especially when I find I've missed an opportunity to complain."

"Not funny, dad," replied Lucy, wearily.

"Well, anyway, I didn't come up here to talk about all of that. I have a little request to make."

Lucy was suspicious, "How little?"

"Oh, well as I see it," began Thomas cautiously, "very little; but you may see it differently of course."

"What is it dad?" demanded Lucy, her arms folded in impatience.

"Your mother and I had a chat earlier today about me helping you out with your running."

"Well, I guess that's kinda ok, as long as you don't expect me to enter into any athletic championships. I especially want nothing to do with that crazy, pathetic, tournament this Saturday, where that horrible little toad Judy Finnimore will be collecting all the medals and cheers."

King Thomas gulped, shuffled uneasily and scratched the back of his head (one of the few places on his head

31

where he still had hair.) "Yes I agree, it would be terrible for that so and so Judy Finnimore to get any more medals and cheers and that's exactly why you must compete on Saturday."

Lucy looked at her father. A mixture of confusion and sadness lined her face, "I'm sorry dad, but I don't see how me finishing last in every race and looking a fool in front of hundreds of people and all my closest friends will help. Surely that will only make Judy look even better?"

"Look, why do you think you would lose every race?" asked the King.

Lucy hung her head, "Let me see now, because I'm about as athletic as an overweight pig."

Thomas tried to reassure her, "But sweetheart, you're not fat and I've seen you run quite swiftly before."

"It's ok dad, I know I'm not fat and that swift running was when I was chasing David, and, well, he isn't even allowed to compete."

The King stood up straight and folded his arms, "Yes, well that may all change," he replied.

"Why? Is David really a girl? I knew there was something odd about him. Wait 'til mum finds out, actually, wait 'til David finds out; he will be surprised... and teased," said Lucy as she enjoyed the thought of her brother suffering.

"No Lucy, David isn't a girl, I mean that much is obvious, you don't name a girl David. Anyway, look at the things he says and does, have you ever seen those from a girl?"

Lucy scrunched up her face in disgust, "Ew yuck, no, thank goodness! Ok, so how will David be able to compete? You're not gonna disguise him as a girl, are you? I know he wouldn't like that, but I would," she giggled.

Thomas looked at his daughter sternly, "No!" He waved his finger at her, "Lucy, your brother has suffered enough at your hands."

Lucy was indignant. "No he hasn't. Just look at what he did to my dolls," she snapped.

"Well, maybe he was trying to improve them? He is only five."

She picked up a doll and angrily held it in front of her father, "Yeah, but look at this one--it's got no head."

Thomas took a good long look at it, "Hey, isn't that the doll you named after yourself?"

"Exactly my point dad," fumed Lucy, "he's vicious!"

Thomas put his hand on his daughter's shoulder and tried to calm her down. "Oh come on sweetheart. He's not vicious." The King sat beside her on the edge of the bed. "He just has some issues to work through, that's all."

Lucy glared at her father. "Dad, he's only five."

"Well, anyway, the way he's gonna compete is by me changing the Royal decree I made, banning males and undesirables from athletics."

"Well, it's true, he is an undesirable. So you want boys and girls to run together?"

Thomas smiled. "Not just boys and girls, but men and women, animals--and even old people."

"Might be a really long race with **very** old people, dad?" laughed Lucy.

The King thought for a moment, "Yeah, better supply them with electric zimmer frames."

"So dad, where do I fit in all of this?"

"Absolutely no pressure Lucy, but if you come first in even one race I will change the law, increase your allowance, and you'll never have to race again."

"Yeah, but you'll have to re-discover your running shoes."

The King was defiant, "No I won't. I'm the king and I'll do as I please."

"If you can do as you please dad, why don't you just **force** me to race on Saturday?"

"Lucy, I can't."

"Why not, dad?"

"I just can't, Lucy."

"Dad, why not?"

"Because, Lucy, I love you."

Lucy's lips began to tremble. She struggled to control her tears. She always knew in her head that her father loved her, but he'd never said it like that before and now she began to know it in her heart. Suddenly, Lucy gave way and started to cry. She knew deep down that now she would do anything to experience her father's love like that again, "Ok, I'll do it, dad."

The King had been startled and rather taken aback by this sudden change of events and felt that he had upset his daughter by his last outburst, "Lucy, I'm sorry."

"I know you are, dad," she replied, gently.

The king softened his voice to almost a whisper, "Thanks sweetheart," he said as he left his daughter's room and made his way into the master bedroom, where his wife lay asleep." She must be exhausted from another day of bright ideas," he thought.

Chapter 2
Shorts

Morning dawned in the Kingdom, greeted steadily and surely by the sound of many fine, and unnecessarily loud, alarm clocks. However, in the bedroom of a certain King, whom we are all now quite familiar with, there was not a whisper or a movement. If there was one thing that the King excelled at it was sleeping. Special servants were required to rouse Thomas and many lost their jobs for 'rousing him too early, even though they would insist that the King specifically told them to wake him at that time.

Today, however, was different. For seemingly out of nowhere came a rushing wind and then a little weight landed on the King and began to shake him, "Come on daddy, today we have to train together. We can start with chicken-throwing if you like and then something more difficult, like running."

"Yes Lucy dear, it's downstairs in the garage," replied the King as he tried to roll over for another bit of sleep.

Lucy looked confused, "What is?"

"The Skipping rope."

"No silly. You said yesterday you would train me for Saturday's championships. You're not backing out are you? I knew it was too good to be true. I knew you'd not do it. You're always the same, you..."

"Alright! Alright! Alright!" snapped Thomas, "I'll be down in a few hours."

"Daddy!" exclaimed Lucy.

"Ok, ok, a few moments," moaned Thomas.

"How long is a moment?"

"Right that does it--I'm up."

The King dragged his irritated self out of bed and headed for the bathroom. Lucy grabbed his arm, "No time for that, dad."

"Yeah, you're probably right. Never bother with it much anyway," he shrugged.

"Here are your clothes, dad."

"I'm not gonna need a tweed suit and a tie to train you in. Where are my shorts?"

"What shorts?" asked Lucy in great surprise. "I've never seen you wearing any before."

"Yes, yes, the little black ones I used to play football in."

Lucy couldn't believe what she was hearing, "Dad, you haven't played football since you were at school!"

"Well, I think we may have a problem then?"

"Why don't you just borrow some from a friend of yours?"

"Good idea Lucy. In fact, I'll just issue a royal decree demanding that all shorts of my measurement be sent to me at once. I'll send it out with my man Godfrey, he'll know what to do."

King Thomas did just that and only one hour later Godfrey returned.

"Well?" demanded Thomas.

"I'm afraid no one is quite," Godfrey gulped; "How should I put this without meaning to offend you sire?"

"I dunno man, just say it as it is," snapped the King.

"Well sire, no one is quite as **fat** as you."

Thomas was furious. "How dare you insult the King. I could have your head for this."

"Well sire, if you had my head you'd certainly be far brainier."

"How dare you, Godfrey! That's it; I will not be insulted by a servant. Guards! Throw this man into the room of musical misery and force him to sing. If he stops, even for a second, make him entertain the kids at the local nursery for a morning. I can't think of anything worse than that. I've seen full grown men keel over at the thought of looking after Harriet and Henry--the terrible twins."

Lucy was stunned, "That was a bit brutal, wasn't it, dad?"

"Yeah, you're right Lucy; I must be merciful. Guards!"

The two guards stopped in their tracks, mere inches from the room of musical misery.

"In discussion with my daughter I have decided to be merciful," announced Thomas. "My servant shall not have to endure that room of musical misery."

Lucy interrupted him, "Dad, why do you call mum's personal movie collection such horrible things?"

"Have you ever seen any of those films, Lucy?"

"No."

"Well, trust me honey, you don't want to. A girl of your age shouldn't be into slushy romantic films or musicals, where every other sentence is some unreasonably happy song."

"Sounds like some of my films."

"Oh no, not two of you," moaned Thomas. "Well, anyway, his punishment has been mercifully adjusted. Though not too harsh, still quite brutal, I think. Godfrey you shall go on a clothes shopping trip with my wife and some of her friends, finished off perhaps with a tedious board game and a whole glass of chocolate milk," declared the King.

This was all too much for poor Godfrey. He threw himself at the King's feet and went into begging mode. "Oh no, please sir! I'll do anything! Please have mercy on me! This punishment is too much for me to bear! You know how long she spends in each shop, picking up everything and then trying it on and on and on and..."

"Alright man, calm yourself. Sheesh! Look, just get me some shorts and we'll call it quits."

"I can't, but isn't it true that your mother-in-law can sew, sire?"

The King's patience was wearing thin; "Yes, but what has that got to do with anything?"

Godfrey stopped trembling, "Well, surely given the right materials could she not make you a pair of shorts?"

"Well, yes, she could, but she's forbidden to work for me by royal decree."

"Could she not teach me?" suggested Godfrey.

"Yes, I suppose so, but she lives far away from here for a very good reason: I don't like her. Thomas leant forward in his chair, menacingly. "Now for goodness sakes don't tell Esmerelda that you're going to see her mother, otherwise she may want her to sew here and when she sews I reap.

Well, to cut an increasingly long story short, we shall fast forward past the King's servant and mother-in-law's shorts making time and stop at the exact moment the servant's return is announced.

"Well?" barked King Thomas, as his main servant Godfrey walked into the Throne Room and bowed.

"I do not have just one pair of shorts for you sire, but two beautifully handcrafted pairs," replied Godfrey with great pride.

The King had no time for pleasantries, "Yes, yes, man--just get one of the pairs out and then I can finally get changed. My daughter's been waiting a good few hours already, any longer and we'll be practising in the dark."

"Very well sire." Godfrey, his hands shaking with fear, gave the carrier bag to his Royal Highness. Snatching the bag in pent-up frustration, the King removed a pair of shorts with a very pretty floral pattern on them. "What is the meaning of this?" he cried, "These are no good. They're women's shorts! I demand an explanation!"

Godfrey was once again emotionally blown apart by the King's great temper, "Well sire...erm...it was your mother-in-law," twitched the servant nervously, "she said that because I came at such short notice all the shops would be shut. This material was all that she had and seeing as you were in such a rush, Your Majesty, I thought it unwise to argue. Please have mercy on me and don't send me to the room of musical misery or on any shopping trips with your wife."

"Well, let's just see if there's a way around this. If I turn them inside out..." As the king turned the shorts inside out, to his horror, they were found to be exactly the same on the inside. "Oh this is ridiculous. It's a jolly conspiracy! I knew she hated me with great passion, now I have the proof."

As Godfrey made his way towards the exit the King arose from his throne and yelled after him, "Right Godfrey, my good man, make a royal declaration! If anyone in the kingdom can make a pair of blue sports shorts, elasticated waist and," the King paused, "waist size reasonably large-ish, they are to start work at dawn and bring the finished products to me ASAP. Failure to receive a pair of blue sports shorts by 10 am tomorrow will result in me increasing taxes and borrowing land willy-nilly all over the place, just for the sake of it, because I'm king. Send that out immediately Godfrey."

Godfrey, the king's ever faithful servant, scurried out of the Throne Room at top speed, which for him was rather slow."

"Hurry up man," yelled the king from behind the exiting old man, to which his response was the commencement of a light skip.

"Lucy honey!" The King called for his daughter as he walked around the darkened castle gardens. Finally, his eyes rested on a little lonely looking figure on the steps of the utility room door. "Lucy sweetheart, it's getting late. Your mum would do the conga 'round the castle if she knew you were still up."

Lucy looked up and chuckled, "Dad, what on earth are you wearing? They're not mum's are they? On second thoughts they can't be, she wouldn't be seen dead in those retros."

The King's reply was rather sarcastic. "No, your very sweet, tasteful, ney tactful, full-on-fun grandmother made them for me. Isn't that sweet of her?"

"No, not really," laughed Lucy, "besides dad, I thought you and grandma didn't get on very well?"

Thomas sighed, "Is it so painfully obvious, even my kids notice?"

"Well dad, you don't exactly hide the fact when you ban someone from coming to see you for more than once a year."

"Yes, I guess that is a slight give-away," agreed the King.

Lucy looked directly into her father's face, "Dad?"

"Yes sweetheart?"

"Do ya think we can make it?"

"No."

The king's answer shocked Lucy. "No!" she gasped.

"No." The King sat down on the step next to her. "I know **YOU** can make it, but as for me I think I'm gonna struggle quite a bit."

"Yeah, especially in those shorts," laughed Lucy, as she got up off the steps and walked with her dad back into the castle. They said their goodnights and Lucy smiled to herself as she thought of her daddy and how he was so concerned with her right now. At last, she was able to spend some quality time with him. Not that she would push the relationship by asking him to help her pick out an athletic outfit in the numerous stores she had in mind. Besides, judging by her father's floral shorts, perhaps it wasn't such a good idea after all.

Chapter 3

Preparations

Shafts of sunlight streamed through the castle windows as a new day dawned in the kingdom of our beloved King Thomas. Unusually, today the King arose first among his family. As he made his way into his daughter's room he found himself whistling a jolly tune. Lucy was awoken from her restful state by the less than melodic sound. "I don't care who you are, but could you please whistle somewhere else?" she moaned.

Thomas was undeterred, "Come on lazy bones, rise and shine. There's a beautiful day dawning outside and we've much to achieve today."

There was a deep groan from the half awake princess, "Exactly dad, it's dawning outside--not in here. Let it dawn itself and we can go out when it's finished its dawning, ok?"

The King began to lose his patience, not to mention his jolly whistle, "That's it young lady, you get out of bed right now! I didn't have my servants put ice cubes in my bed this morning to wake me up just so that I could watch you sleep all morning. If you don't get up in the next five minutes I shall be forced to...erm...well...erm."

"It's ok dad, you can keep whatever it was you were so eagerly thinking of threatening me with to yourself," said Lucy as she clambered out of bed and headed towards her private bathroom. On the way she caught sight of the clock, "Dad, it's 6:30!"

"I know. I'm sorry I'm a little later than I'd planned to be. I feel like I let the side down a bit."

"No worries about that dad, trust me." Lucy stopped just before the bathroom and turned to face her dad, "I thought you loved sleep more than anything else in the world though?"

"No sweetheart, I have my priorities and this, you, are more important."

Lucy gulped and tried to hold back any emotion that might embarrass her father. She wondered who had run off with her daddy and how long this stranger, who looked and sounded like him, would be here. Since when did he get up for anything or anyone? Even waffles with caramella custard were ignored and eventually binned so he could finish off an interesting dream. He really had changed, but for how long?

Some time later, Thomas knocked on his daughter's bathroom door. "Lucy, are you gonna be in there forever and a day?" he asked.

"At least I wash!" came the reply.

"I'll be downstairs in the Rose Garden. You have two minutes and I mean 120 seconds, not a second more, not a second less, understand?"

"Yes, ok, yada, yada, yada," came the nonchalant reply.

Ten minutes later, that is 600 seconds, or 480 seconds longer than she was supposed to be, Lucy emerged from the castle and into the Rose Garden, where her ever-patient father sat picking off petals. Lucy appeared confused by his strange behaviour; "What are you doing, dad?" she asked.

"Oh nothing really. Just playing a slightly different version of the game, 'He loves me. He loves me not,' but instead it goes, 'she will come down, she'll come down not.'"

Lucy wasn't impressed; "Alright, alright, ha, ha, dad."

"Ok are we honey-bunch?"

She glared at her father. "Dad, don't call me that!"

"Well, would you prefer snookums, deary or sweetypie?"

"No, but how about Lucy?"

"Touchy, aren't we? Well, never mind, I now have my blue sports shorts; what do ya think?" said Thomas as he attempted a little jog.

"A bit small aren't they?"

"Oh it's all the rage now, short shorts."

Lucy rolled her eyes. "Whatever you say dad."

"Anyway, rather than roam around the kingdom looking for people who might be able to help you train, I thought I'd look in the Fellow Pages for some help," said Thomas as he produced a brightly coloured book.

"You always look in that book, but it's only men in there."

Thomas looked surprised. "What's wrong with that?"

"Well, seeing as men aren't even allowed to take part in any athletic activity and I'm a girl, we should look in this."

Lucy handed her father a small book filled with information.

Thomas seemed rather surprised, "Your mother's phone diary thingy?"

"Yes, I know it's not officially endorsed by you," laughed Lucy, "but every woman in the kingdom has one."

"Well, let's have a look...oh I don't know any of these people."

Lucy put her hands on her hips and sighed; "It might help if you weren't reading it upside down, dad."

The king turned the little book around the right way; "No, I still don't recognise anyone."

"Shall I organise my trainers?" asked Lucy.

"Yes, it's about time you sorted out your shoes."

"No, I mean people who will train me."

"No sweetheart, it's ok, I'll organise it. While I do I want you to run from here to Lake Lamondise and back and I'll see what time you make it in, ok?"

"Oh, ok," replied Lucy, and sped off at the pace of a seriously injured snail, while the king headed towards his specially designed private phone booth.

It was quite some time later that an out of breath Lucy returned to the castle, ready to collapse. The Queen, who was taking a stroll in the garden, suddenly caught sight of her daughter and rushed over with great concern; "Are you alright sweetypie?"

Lucy couldn't speak; she just nodded.

"Were you running in training for Saturday?"

Lucy nodded.

"Was it your father's idea?"

Lucy nodded.

"Should I be merciful to him?"

Lucy shook her head.

"Come on sweetheart, I'll run you a nice warm bath with plenty of bubbles and you can just relax, you poor thing."

Esmerelda almost carried Lucy into the house and up to the bath.

Leaving her daughter to soak, the Queen made her way to where her husband was telephoning as many people as he could, in as short a time as was humanly possible. She waited for him to end his current conversation, and then began to yell, "Thomas, why is our daughter half dead?"

The King smiled, "Oh, she's back? Good, now I can check what time it took her."

"Oh yes she's back, whatever's left of her. Where did you tell her to run to?" exclaimed the Queen.

"Oh...erm..." Thomas shuffled uneasily, "just to the lake and back."

"Which lake?"

"Oh you know," Thomas continued his uneasy shuffling, "Lake Lamondise."

The Queen simply exploded, "Lake Lamondise!!! That's five miles away."

"Really? I would never have thought it that far," gulped the king in surprise.

Esmerelda calmed herself down and put her arm around Thomas; "Look dear, I know you always mean well, in your heart, but she's only a child and five miles is more than any of the youngsters are expected to run, in any athletic event. If you were struggling with the whole training thing why didn't you just ask me to do it with you, we are a team, ya know?"

"You're right, honey. I have been a bit foolish in all of this."

Esmerelda looked at her husband kindly. "That's ok sweetheart," she smiled.

"So...erm--got any ideas?" asked Thomas, tentatively.

"Not yet," laughed the Queen, "but give me a bit of time and I'll put my little grey cells through their paces and see what I can come up with." With that last piece of wonderful encouragement, she left the king and headed towards her study.

Moments later Thomas was awoken from his unintentional nap by his loving and ever patient wife. She had an idea, but it was going to mean a lot of hard work and a very open mind.

"Here in my hand is a list. On the left hand side of the list are the events Lucy should train for. On the right hand are, what I consider, the best people to help her in each of the events. All I need is your Royal seal of approval and they will all be here in the morning," announced the Queen.

"You have it my dear, you have it," said Thomas as he rolled over and continued his beloved snooze, much to his wife's annoyance. She would now have to wait until he had finished his nap before anything was signed, and it was only three days until the athletic tournament.

Chapter 4

Princess in Training

A bright and sunny Wednesday morning dawned, much to Lucy's dismay. She was still tired from yesterday's exhausting run and wondered what pleasures her father had in store for her today. The only thing she knew was that there would be no crazy runs to any far away lakes, that's for certain.

"Morning pumpkin!" chirped the King.

"Yes I know," moaned Lucy.

"Oh, well look, don't be like that. Imagine all the fun we're gonna have today."

Lucy just glared at him. So, Thomas attempted to smooth things over; "Look, I know yesterday was a bit too much for you dear and I apologise for my oversight, but today will be different, I promise."

"A bit too much!" cried Lucy in shock. "I can hardly move today because of you."

"Well, yes, anyway. Boria the chicken-throwing champion and Deirdre the jumper are waiting downstairs."

"Wow dad, hold me back please!" replied Lucy sarcastically.

"Yes, quite, well, I'll be waiting downstairs. Try not to be too long honey."

"Yeah, yeah, ok," came the tired reply.

Lucy threw on some clothes and made her way downstairs in the manner of a poor convicted criminal on her way to the gallows.

"Ah, here's my little joy of summer!" said Thomas, as Lucy exited the castle and dragged herself over to the drawbridge.

To cut a long story short, which of course I must, Lucy tried the ancient art of chicken-throwing. To avoid any cruelty to animals this event was performed using rubber chickens. She hurled them with all her strength, but just couldn't get a decent distance, in fact, one poor chicken was never found again, but then it was only rubber. Boria was paid for her time and her missing chickens. She went home shaking her head in simple disbelief. Next was Deirdre-the jumper. The winner of this athletic challenge would be the one who was still jumping when the music stopped. Lucy didn't even get past the first verse before giving up and although Deirdre insisted on jumping through a few more songs the king was having none of it and took the batteries out of her turntable.

"Oh this is stupid, daddy," moaned Lucy. "There's no point in pretending anymore. It's obvious I can't compete on Saturday, you'll just have to find someone else."

Thomas sighed; "Well, even though I'm as stubborn as a bull and hate quitting once I've begun, I have to agree with you on this one."

The King put his hand on his daughter's shoulder as he passed her by. Then he went back into the castle. Lucy sat outside and cried.

As the King entered the Throne Room he immediately saw his beautiful wife, Queen Esmerelda. She was watching one of her favourite films, which of course, Thomas despised. He sat down on his Throne next to her and stared into space. The Queen leant over to her husband and asked; "What's the matter sweetheart? You look glum."

"I am. I got a couple of the greatest athletes here, as you suggested, and Lucy just, well, she just wasn't up to scratch that's all."

"Well, that doesn't really surprise me sweetheart," sighed the Queen, "I mean you can't exactly force someone who hates, and therefore never practices, athletics to suddenly be good enough to compete. Good trainers or not, she's her own person with her own unique skills. Perhaps throwing chickens and jumping to music is just not her thing. Maybe, just maybe, you should try looking at what she's already good at, rather than trying to train her to do something new?"

"How am I supposed to do that, exactly?" asked Thomas in frustration.

"Observe her and see what she does privately, in her own time and space."

The king's eyebrows arched in disbelief; "You want me to spy on my own daughter?"

"No, just spend time with her--you know, 'hanging out.'"

"Hanging out?" mocked the King; "I hardly think that's appropriate."

"That's the trouble then, isn't it? You're too busy being king that you don't leave enough time to be dad. You can get others to run your kingdom for you, but you can't get others to be a father to your daughter--she needs you!"

With his wife's friendly advice still ringing in his ears, the King made his way outside to find his daughter and maybe, just maybe, a little more of himself as well.

"Hi honey," said the King as he approached the castle steps where his daughter was reading a book.

Lucy looked weary, "Hi daddy," she replied.

The King peered over her shoulder, "What ya reading?"

Lucy seemed embarrassed and fumbled around trying to cover up the title of her book. "Oh, it's nothing really," she said.

"Can I have a look, honey?"

Lucy shrugged and handed over the book, "Erm...ok... I guess?"

Thomas read the title aloud; "'The Art of Chicken-Throwing and Its Place in Modern Junior Athletics.' Sounds like a heavy read?"

"Yeah," agreed Lucy, "it's really boring."

The King put the book down and sat next to his daughter; "Look sweetheart, you don't have to study chicken-throwing or any other athletics. I never even bothered to ask you what you wanted. I just assumed that, as your King and father, I could just demand things of you willy-nilly and you'd obey me like one of my common servants, but you're not one of my servants, you're my daughter and as such should be given a bit more respect. I know it's right that you obey me, but it's not right for me to use you for my own selfish ways."

Lucy just sat there stunned and shocked. She was really worried about her dad's state of mind. Sure she preferred this version of her father to the old one, but how long would it last and did he have secret motives behind all of the niceness?

"I know what you're thinking," said Thomas.

Lucy was shocked; "You do?"

"Yes, you're thinking that I'm being nice because I want something--and I'm afraid you're right."

Lucy jumped to her feet; her long blonde hair flew everywhere as she literally shook with rage; "Oh I just knew this was too good to be true! I knew you'd recover from your niceness disease sooner or later! I knew..."

"Lucy, please let me finish. All I want from you is your company."

Lucy was confused; "My company? I don't have a company, I'm a royal Princess."

"No, no, sweetie," laughed Thomas, "not that type of company. I just wanna hang out with you."

Lucy sat back down on the steps; "No way dad. I have an image to think about."

"Well, it doesn't have to be all the time Lucy, just when you'll let me."

She was a little suspicious of her father's new offer; "Are you serious dad? Is that really all you want? Are you sure there's nothing else? Are you sure you don't want me to compete on Saturday?"

"I'd love for you to compete on Saturday, but only if **you** want to," smiled the King.

"Ok, ok, dad you can hang out with me, but I might watch films you don't like and listen to music you usually torture your enemies with," warned Lucy.

"Yes, I'm well aware of the risks," replied Thomas as he 'rose to his feet, "but I'm willing to suffer a little just to be with you."

Lucy smiled and swallowed back any emotions that might embarrass her. As her father left to go back inside, she called out to him, "Dad?"

The King stopped and turned to face her.

"Thanks," she said.

Later, that self-same day, the King entered his daughter's room.

"It's ok dad, you can take them off," giggled Lucy, "I'm not gonna play any of my music while you're in here."

The King took the fluffy earmuffs off and began to inspect his daughter's room, secretly hoping to find some evidence of athletic talent. He found none. Then an idea struck him. Noticing his daughter's extensive film and music collections, the little grey cells started whirring.

"You must have **all** the albums by Boyfluff," said Thomas.

"No, they have a new one out soon. In fact I think it's out today, but I can't afford it."

"That's a shame. Not enough pocket money, eh?"

Lucy picked up the most beautiful and well cared for items in the room, "No, spent it all on these."

"On just one pair of shoes?" asked Thomas in surprise.

"Yes, well, it's not like you'd get two pairs for the amount of gold you give me," complained Lucy.

"Well, I think the shops are about 800 metres away, but if I gave you the money and you were quick enough you might be able to get Boyfluff's new album before closing time. Bearing in mind that they shut in less than five minutes."

"Oh daddy. Yes please!" Lucy held out her hand and Thomas thrust a bit of gold into it.

"Now off you go, hurry, as quick as you can," said King Thomas as he looked at the time on his watch.

As soon as his daughter had left, the King telephoned the music store and told them to let him know the exact time, to the second, that Lucy arrived. He made it clear that if this were not done for him there would be severe consequences.

Breathless, but still full of energy, Lucy returned to the castle--without a Boyfluff album.

"They'd completely sold out and now I'll just have to wait until the next time you feel generous," said Lucy, as she handed her father the gold coins.

Just then, the King's phone started to ring. He picked it up. It was the music store. They had recorded his daughter's time upon reaching them.

"Are you quite sure?" asked the king, rather surprised by the time quoted to him.

"I'll be in my room, dad," said a tired and weary Lucy.

"Ok Lucy. I'm sorry about the Boyfluff album."

"Yeah, I know, I know," replied Lucy with great sadness as she clumped up the stairs.

Thomas finished his conversation with the music store and wandered into his wife's study.

"Hello darling, have you had a good day?" asked the Queen, as she embraced her husband.

"Yes. Did you know that Lucy ran 800 metres in just over three and a half minutes?"

"No sweetheart," laughed the Queen, "no one her age has ever run the 800 metres in that time. It's impossible."

"No seriously. She ran to the music store and back in three minutes and thirty-three seconds. The shop swears by it and I know what time she left here."

"If that's true, then she's far faster than Judy Finnimore--the regional champion. Her best time is four minutes and eighteen seconds. You set her up Thomas, didn't you?"

The King's chest puffed out with pride, "Why, yes I did," he replied smugly.

"You genius, Thomas," said Esmerelda as she gave her husband a kiss.

"First time I've ever been called that," he laughed.

"You must try to convince her to enter on Saturday. With a time like that, she cannot lose."

Moments after their conversation, the King left his wife and tried to get the attention of his daughter who was in her bedroom upstairs; "Lucy, can you come down here for a moment sweetheart?" he yelled.

"What is it?" she yelled back.

The King prepared to yell again; "Did you know that you're the fastest junior 800 metres runner in the region?"

"And did you know, dad, that those sorts of lies will not convince me to make a fool of myself on Saturday?"

Thomas yelled yet again; "It's no lie. I have evidence. You ran all the way to the store today for the Boyfluff album, didn't you?"

" No, I walked some of the way too," came the returning yell.

"Wow, even better then," yelled the King.

"Sorry?" yelled Lucy.

"Stop yelling Lucy and come down here. The person writing this story has to write that we yelled after every yell and he's quite fed up with all the yelling. So, come down here so we don't have to yell anymore," yelled the King.

Much to both the King and author's delight, Lucy made her way downstairs and into her father's study.

As she entered, her father spoke; "This is how long it took you." The King showed his daughter a piece of paper with her time on it. "And this..." Thomas produced an official document, "is the certificate of the winner of last year's 800 metres championship. Notice the time. Notice the name."

Lucy was astonished; "Are you telling me that the great Judy Finnimore is slower than me?"

"No, she's only slower than you when you put your heart and soul into a run."

"You mean she's only slower than me when I'm running for the latest Boyfluff album?" laughed Lucy.

"Well, on the evidence of today, I'd say yes."

"So, if I go up against her on Saturday with no Boyfluff album to get before closing time, I could lose?"

"No, because I'm gonna give you an even greater reason to win," smiled Thomas.

Lucy scratched her head; "How can there be an even greater reason than the latest Boyfluff album?"

"If you go up against Judy Finnimore on Saturday in the 800 metres, win or lose, I will give you a gift that far exceeds any Boyfluff album ever released."

Lucy was astonished, "What?"

"I cannot spoil the surprise, but please trust me on this, even if you never trust me with anything else again."

"Ok, but don't let me down dad; I'm counting on you, big time."

Thomas held out his hand, "Do we have a deal then?"

"We have a deal," said Lucy, as she took hold of her father's hand and gave it a good shake."

Chapter 5
The Race

Later that day, the King spoke privately on the phone, "Hello, is this the manager of Boyfluff?"

"It's six in the morning," replied the man wearily.

"I'm well aware of the time my good man, but you haven't answered my question," snapped the King.

"Who is this?"

"This is his Royal loftiness King Thomas."

"Is this some kind of joke?" asked the manager, rather upset.

"I beg your pardon?" replied the King, quite offended.

The manager was still very suspicious, "Are you **really** King Thomas?"

"Yes I am."

"Then I'm probably in deep brown stuff, aren't I?" gulped the manager. "Otherwise, why would you call?"

"Actually, I'm calling to book your band."

"Which one? I manage several and if you want The Tribal Monkeys or Lullaby Slashed they're fully booked."

"Who on earth would want them?" asked the King in great surprise; "No, I'm after booking Boyfluff."

"Ah yes, but I wouldn't 'ave thought they were your type of band."

"No, not for me. For my daughter."

The Boyfluff manager swung his leather office chair around to view his calendar, and after a quick flick through the months, he replied; "Well, I think they're already booked for the rest of the year."

"No they're not. They're free on Saturday. In fact, I believe that the very King who holds your wage and licence in his most noble hands has booked them to cheer his daughter Lucy on in the Regional Junior Athletics Championships. My man Godfrey will deliver to you the exact instructions for Saturday and the penalties should any of those instructions be ignored. Do we have an understanding?" threatened the King.

The manager sighed; "Yeah, I guess we do."

"I know I was being a bit pushy and demanding, but that's all part of the job of a king in the middle ages."

"But we're not in the middle ages," replied the manager, rather confused.

"I know but I'm middle aged, which I guess is my point."

The manager of Boyfluff held his head in his hands and sighed; "Whatever you say, Your Majesty."

"My friends call me Thomas."

"Oh sorry, Thomas."

"Now what gave you the idea you were my friend?"

"Sorry, Your Majesty," moaned the manager.

"That's more like it. Remember my instructions must be obeyed or the only music you'll be hearing will be from the room of musical misery. Understand?" There was a gulp and a stammered, "Yes," from the Boyfluff manager.

Just then Lucy emerged from the bathroom, towel-drying her locks and whistling a tune the King thought rather vulgar. Coincidentally, it was a Boyfluff tune. She walked over to her father and tapped him on the shoulder, "Who was that you were talking to daddy?"

"Oh nobody important. Let's just say it was the Prime Minister, for arguments sake."

"Oh no, not him again," chuckled Lucy. "He's always asking for money or your signature on something. What was it he wanted last time he called?"

"My head on a new set of, what they're calling, postage stamps. It'll never catch on. No one will ever abandon their faithful carrier pigeons."

Suddenly, Lucy became quite serious; "Dad, do you think I'll make it on Saturday?"

The King looked confused; "Yeah of course, I'll make sure the Royal carriage picks you up."

"No, I mean do you think I can win the 800 metres race?"

"My darling, if I didn't think you could win I wouldn't even bother to enter you. In my eyes you have already won, no matter what the result ends up being."

Lucy gave her dad a peck on the cheek and skipped outside to practise. In fact, she practised regularly every day leading up to the championships.

Finally, Saturday dawned. Lucy leapt out of bed, which was about as usual for her as it would be for a lemming not to jump if pushed to the edge of a cliff. She had already prepared her sports outfit the night before, and once ready she went outside to do some warm up exercises her mum had shown her. Lucy was delighted when her dad, who never usually rode with her in the same carriage, insisted upon escorting her to the tournament. He encouraged and flattered his daughter all the way, until it became too much for her. She had found her biggest fan. A fan that had kept so quiet all of her life thus far.

Upon arrival at the athletic grounds, Lucy noticed lots of scarves and hats with her name on them.

"So many people are wearing scarves and hats on a blazing hot summer's day, it worries me, and they look like the kind of garment only grandma could make," said Lucy.

"Yeah, she wouldn't do them for me, but when I mentioned that it was for you, she just couldn't help herself."

"It's a really nice idea dad, thanks."

Lucy and her father sat in the stands while the many other athletic events went on. She clutched her daddy's hand for comfort. Her heart was racing; she had butterflies.

Lucy had never been so nervous. The King squeezed her hand and tried to re-assure her, "Darling, I know you can do this. I believe in you and remember, no matter what happens out there; I will never allow you to be looked down upon. You will always be a champion to me."

Lucy managed a half smile. However much she had warmed to her father's words they could not replace the feelings of utter nervousness she felt. Lucy went to the side of the track to warm up and then it was time for her to line up with the rest of the girls at the starting line. The moment had come and now there was no going back.

Lucy shook as she waited for the sound of the starters gun. Suddenly, "bang!" and they were off. Lucy launched herself forward with an almighty heave ho only to, at the same moment, catch sight of a small blonde girl with neat little pigtails and covered in the pinkest of clothes.

"Judy Finnimore. Oh how I hate her," thought Lucy and as she thought that very thought she noticed, to her delight, the finish line.

Suddenly, Judy Finnimore tripped over her own shoelaces and landed flat on her face, inches from the finish line. Lucy couldn't believe her good fortune. Here was her chance, her only chance. Her moment of sweet revenge. So why on earth was she stopping while all the other girls ran past her? Was she tired? No, she seemed to have boundless energy. Lucy came to a standstill where her archenemy, the girl she despised, lay helpless and utterly humiliated. Suddenly, she found herself stretching out her hand to the girl she had never liked. Judy grabbed it and was hoisted up. The crowd cheered, but Lucy couldn't hear them. Not that they were cheering for her. For Judy and Lucy were joint losers and no one could take that away from them. Lucy sat Judy down by the side of the track and they both watched as the other girls were all congratulated and made to feel special.

"They deserve it, I guess," said Lucy sadly.

Judy turned and looked her in the face, "No, you deserve it. Why did you stop and help me? I thought you hated me?"

"I did, and I don't really know why I helped you. My dad always says that no one is actually good. People just do good things from time to time. I think he says it as an excuse to mum, but I've never done anything for anyone I hated before," she paused, "well, nothing nice that is."

"Why did you hate me?" asked Judy.

Lucy shrugged, "I dunno. I guess I was jealous because you're always the best at everything."

"I'm not today, am I?" replied Judy, as a tear fell from her eye.

Lucy put her arm around her; "Hey, it was an accident."

"Yeah, like all my friends are gonna see it that way." Judy held her head in her hands; "I'm such a loser now."

"Well, join the club," said Lucy.

"What are you talking about?" asked Judy looking up in great surprise. "You're a princess. You have everything money can buy."

"Yeah, but none of that matters really. The only thing I ever wanted was love, especially from my dad and then from people at school."

"Well, trust me Lucy, it's hard work gaining their love. The people at school love you only if you look, talk and act right. I know; I'm a pro at it. As for my dad," Judy hung her head, "well I miss him, he's been dead for a while now."

"Oh I'm sorry Judy, I really am. Look, if you wanna be my friend, my castle drawbridge is always down for you."

Judy laughed, "Thanks, I guess it's a bit better than our three bedroom semi-detached."

Suddenly, Judy's mother came across to her. "Are you alright? What have I told you about making sure your laces are tied tightly?" she snapped.

"I know mum," whimpered Judy, "I'm sorry."

Judy's mother, oblivious to her daughter's apology, continued to rant and rave, "There was absolutely no reason to lose that race, young lady. Now what am I going to do? We'll be a laughing stock and I have an image to uphold."

"Mum, this is Lucy," said Judy, desperately trying to change the subject.

"Oh how lovely," replied Judy's mother sarcastically, "the King's daughter. Well, at least you did one thing right today." She grabbed her daughter roughly by the arm, "Come along Judy, let's be off home before I have to face the music."

After the way Judy's mother had been, Lucy wondered if she might receive the same treatment from her dad,

"Was he really a changed man? He had been reading books recently, which wasn't like him."

Just then, a burly man with a curly black moustache interrupted her thoughts, "Young lady, you cannot sit here all day."

"That's my daughter and she can sit wherever she likes, whenever she likes, for as long as she likes."

"Yeah and who are you, the King or somethin'?" laughed the burly man.

"Actually yes," replied Thomas as he waved his Royal signet ring in front of the policeman.

"Oh...erm...begging your pardon sire."

"Yes, yes, just get outa here," said the King, as he brushed the man aside.

Lucy began to apologise, "Daddy, I messed up. I lost the race. I..."

The King put his finger gently over her mouth, "Shhh honey. Don't you know that I don't care about that? Don't you know that I said before the race even began that no matter what happens here today you will still be my champion? What you did for your enemy, Judy Finnimore, I wouldn't have even done and I'm the King and should know a lot better. You showed, by sacrificing the race and your reputation to help someone you didn't even like, the true heart of a champion."

The King sat down on the grass next to his daughter, "Even if you had come first and not stopped to help Judy, my love for you would remain the same."

Lucy was shocked, "Why dad? Who have you been talking to? What have you been reading? Did you bang your head?"

"No," laughed Thomas, "none of those things. I just had a change of heart. I only realised my neglect of you when I remembered my own dad's neglect of me. I felt helpless. I didn't wanna treat you the same as he did me and yet found myself treating you in even worse ways. Then one night, I got on my knees and cried out in prayer." The King smiled, "You know me Lucy; I've never been a God-fearing man. I've never really needed Him, to be honest, but I didn't wanna lose you and I was willing to try anything and anyone. You know what it's like in these fairy tales, the King always seeks the wrong advice and somebody becomes a frog or something, or the girl seeks out her wicked stepmother and gets turned into a pumpkin."

"Er, dad, I think you've got that wrong," suggested Lucy.

"Yes, you're right, I think it wasn't a pumpkin, but a horse she was turned into and then the horse had to kiss the prince, who was a dwarf anyway."

"Oh dear, dad," laughed Lucy, "you really aren't in with the fairy tale crew."

"No, well, anyway, I thought why didn't these people try God? He is the biggest and most powerful, after all. I knew He didn't use magic, but I thought I'd give Him a call."

Lucy leant forward, "Was He in?"

"Remarkably I don't know, but I do know one thing; I've jolly well changed towards you, haven't I Lucy?"

"You sure have dad, but I've been worried as to whether it would last."

"Me too," agreed Thomas, "I mean it's certainly not automatic. I have to make the right decisions, but I just feel quite assisted and full of good ideas, that's all."

"Well dad, if you last like this into the next story, without too many relapses, I might actually take the time to make the call to the unseen one myself."

"Oh, are you coming to this sweetheart?"

The King handed a flyer to Lucy which read, 'Royal Boyfluff concert in celebration of Princess Lucy. Straight after the athletic championships, once everyone's caught their breath and paid ridiculous amounts for overpriced beverages and food.'

"Oh daddy!" Lucy threw her arms around her dad and then proceeded to jump up and down with extra sensory excitement.

The concert was a wonderful occasion and once summer was over and a new term began at Oakswell School, Lucy sought out and found, her new friend, Judy. They were far from losers after the concert organised by King Thomas, but they knew that the newfound admiration was shallow. They enjoyed it while it lasted and then shrugged their shoulders, smiled and whistled down the road, as Lucy thought of her father and her father thought of how lucky he was not to have to compete in anything athletic himself.

The End.

King Thomas the Adventurer in....

HEADS TOGETHER NOW

Chapter One
Esmerelda leaves

A new day dawned in the Kingdom as King Thomas rolled over for another bit of sleep. Just then, a cry came from downstairs, "Wake up lazy bones!"

"How rude!" thought the King and shouted back, "No!"

"But, you said you'd start a war today."

"I've changed my mind," yelled Thomas.

"You can't, you've already declared it and there's some men waiting outside."

This surprised the King and he sat up in bed, "Really?" he replied.

"Yes."

The King arose from bed and put on his finest military garb. He marched downstairs, as a general of the highest degree, clump, clump, clump. At the bottom of the staircase he met his wife, Queen Esmerelda.

"Morning sweetheart, your porridge is on the table," said the Queen, cheerfully.

"Never mind about that. Where are my recruits?"

The King made his way out into the courtyard to find...nobody. He marched back into the kitchen and sat in front of his porridge; "Where are they Esmerelda?" he snapped.

The Queen shuffled uneasily, "Well...erm...ok, I lied. I had to get you out of bed somehow. You're taking me shopping, remember?"

The King was enraged; "How dare you lie to me, I'm not taking you shopping now! You'll just have to find someone else to borrow money from."

"But, you're the King," moaned Esmerelda, "all the money comes from you. Besides which, you promised you would take me."

The King was incredulous, "When did I promise that?"

"Last week sometime."

Thomas threw his hands in the air, "Oh how am I supposed to remember that?"

"If it was important to you, you'd remember," sighed Esmerelda; "you always remember the things that matter to you."

"Well that's true, I suppose. Look, I try my level best to escape shopping trips. I hate them," the King shivered, "they bring me out in lumps and bumps. Allergic reactions, I think?"

Esmerelda looked sad, "Don't you wanna spend time with me though?" she asked. "I suggest shopping and you say no. I suggest movies and you say no. The only things you say yes to are the ones tailor made for you."

"Again very true, but as king I have obligations. After all, if the King is not rested how will he make accurate decisions? If I'm absolutely stressed out from a shopping trip or all emotional after a movie I'll be too unstable to rule well."

The Queen rolled her eyes, sighed, and put her hands on her hips, "What absolute nonsense Thomas," she blasted, "you're just selfish, that's all. Plain selfish. Yes I like shopping with my friends, without our men in the way, but I'd also like to do things with you, that I enjoy."

Esmerelda walked over to her husband; "Do you see where I'm coming from?" she asked.

"No, not really," replied Thomas, "but to be a good queen you mustn't complain so much about the actions and inactions of your king."

"Look Thomas, I know as arranged marriages go we've made it work, it's just that I'm so tired of it all being about you. I'm going away for the weekend to Nadi's house and I'll see if you can have a think about us, instead of you, for a change."

"Yeah," agreed the King, "the break might do you good, give you a chance to relax and chill out."

The Queen could not believe what she was hearing, "Oh my gosh! You just can't see yourself, can you?"

"Why? Does my reflection look off this morning?" asked Thomas, rather confused.

Esmerelda gave him a quick peck on the cheek, "Ok honey, never mind."

That Friday afternoon the King waved goodbye to his Queen as she left in the Royal carriage, accompanied by several guards and assistants.

"House to myself. Oh joy, joy, house to myself." The King was in the most jovial of moods, that is, until he realised that he had his two children to look after. Just then, his thoughts were interrupted by a knock on the door. It was Agnes Andersaan the Dutch nanny, who he'd forgotten he even had.

"I've come to collect the children, sire," said Agnes.

"Oh yes, jolly good," replied Thomas, rubbing his hands with glee.

"I'm to take them to Nico and Nadi's for the weekend and look after them there," Agnes cleared her throat. "That is, if you agree?"

"Yes, might as well, seeing as you've come all this way."

Agnes looked bemused; "I live in the left wing of your castle, sire."

"Oh yes, the left wing. Is that the west wing?" asked Thomas.

"No, it's the wing you keep the birds in."

"Oh, the chicken wing." said Thomas with a smile.

Agnes tried to hide her distaste for the King's poor humour. "Very amusing, your Highness," she replied, dryly.

"Well, I try, you know."

"So, if you don't mind me asking, what will you be doing this weekend, Your Majesty?"

"Eating, drinking, merriment. What else is there? Might start that war I've been meaning to begin with our neighbours to the south, if I can get enough people interested."

Agnes suddenly looked worried. "You mean the Baxter's, sire?"

"Yes, that whole housing estate," said the King as he pointed southwards. "I don't like them, to be perfectly honest. Loud music, strange little habits and, above all, a shopping centre that consists of the most abhorrently boring stores."

"My sister Agnalia and her husband Brian live there, sire."

Thomas did not appear to be worried, "Oh, that is unfortunate. Well, I probably won't do too much damage if they surrender quickly."

With that, the conversation between the King and his children's nanny was over.

"I might as well head back to bed," thought Thomas, as he gave a small yawn.

Meanwhile, the Queen had arrived at Nico and Nadi's tent in the Forest of Excitement. Nadi was delighted to see her friend and spoke of all the wonderful things they would do on their weekend together. She explained that her husband Nico had gone off to see King Thomas. The two women conversed about their husbands and about life in general. They laughed, chatted and generally had a whale of a time that first night. What a relaxing break from all the stresses of family life. Nadi agreed that Thomas was definitely in the wrong, but what could be done to help him see the error of his ways? She suggested a good marriage counsellor, but Esmerelda just knew that Thomas would never agree.

"Well, if he were married to me, he would jolly well do as he was told," snapped Nadi; "I don't let Nico get away with all that."

Esmerelda looked concerned; "Do you think I'm too soft on him Nadi?"

"Well, yes, but what can you do? He is the King and as such could have you beheaded for even questioning his authority."

The Queen was shocked by her friend's suggestion; "Thomas would never do that. He loves me. He just doesn't see past the end of his nose so often."

Chapter Two
Nico's visit

As the King snoozed in the upper chambers of his luxury castle, there was a sudden knock at the door. Unfortunately, the knock was not nearly loud enough to awaken the King and even if it had been, he would not have got up to open the front door. Thankfully, one of the King's many loyal and stressed out servants went and opened it. Outside stood a brightly clad figure with brightly coloured hair, brightly coloured shoes and a brightly coloured pair of tickets.

"Good morning, sir. Is His Highness expecting you?" asked the King's servant.

"No, he never expects me, that's what's so downright exciting about my visits!"

"Well, you see, the King is sleeping right now and becomes very angry if awoken," warned the servant.

"Oh, he's always sleeping. He's on semi-permanent sleeping pills, if you ask me. Those are not multi-vitamins by the side of his bed, you know."

"Right, well, if you will wait there one moment. Who shall I say, to the potential shortening of my life, is enquiring of His Majesty?"

"Just say it's his friend Nico, he'll know who I am."

"Is that Lord Nico?"

"No, but that would be rather exciting. You can call me Nico the Excitable, but I'm just Nico really."

With that last bit of jolly explanation still ringing in his ears the servant of the King made his way to the upper chambers, and towards the slumbering monarch. In hushed tones he tried to 'rouse the King, but to no avail. Finally, he blew the Kings Shofar. Thomas leapt out of bed and stood to attention, ready for battle. When he realised that no war was forthcoming and he had stood to attention in his underpants, in front of a very nervous servant, he was far less than amused. The King called for his guards. "Before you throw him into prison let this pesky servant of mine tell me his so very important reason for awakening me at only eleven in the morning, on a work day?"

"Y...Y...Your Highness," stammered the servant, "there is a man at the door who goes by the name of Nico and says that he is a friend of yours."

The King sat up, "Not Nico the Excitable?"

"Y...Yes, sire."

"My wife's just gone to stay with his wife for the weekend, maybe that's why he's called 'round. Well, I can't be anti-social, even if it is Nico. Guards, release this servant and tell Nico I will be down in a jiffy."

After a jiffy had passed the King met with Nico and they sat down with a beer in each hand and a smile on each face.

"So, how are you doing sir King and all that?" asked Nico as he took a swig of beer and wiped his mouth in satisfaction.

"Not bad thanks Nico, wife's left me, kids 'ave left me, but that's to be expected, I suppose."

"Yes, rather an exciting experience by the sounds of it?"

"No, rather boring really," replied the King, glumly.

"Oh dear. Well, my wife chucked me out. She's chatting with your Esmerelda. Goodness knows what they talk about, you know?"

"Probably us," said Thomas.

"Yeah, probably."

"How wonderful we are, Nico, to let them have a relaxing weekend all to themselves with the kids, without making any demands on them."

"Yes, we are rather good to them Thomas, it is true."

Meanwhile, back at Nadi's house...

"Well, yes, Nico's the same," complained Nadi. "He always thinks he's doing me a favour when he goes out and leaves me alone. He says that because he loves me he's giving me some space to relax by myself. How can I relax with a couple of screaming kids and a load of housework? I mean, at least you have servants to do your housework and look after your kids."

"Yes that's true Nadi," agreed the Queen, "but I'd still like to know who the husband is beneath the King. He has time for kingly pursuits, but he doesn't see me as one of them."

Nadi took her hand in sympathy, "I know what you mean, luvvie."

Back at the castle...

"Yes, they're lucky to have us. Never hear a complaint out of them, Nico. We really do know about success when it comes to running a family."

"Yes, oh yes we do, Thomas."

"What are those?" asked the king, as he pointed to the brightly coloured pieces of card on the table next to his friend.

"Oh yes," said Nico, "those are tickets for one of the old rock bands we used to like when we had less of a receding hairline."

"Who?" asked the King. "I liked quite a few of them back then?"

"ADFD."

"No way!" replied Thomas in shock. "They're still going? They must be on zimmer frames or something."

Nico reached for his beer. "No, they're still quite fit for their age," he said as he took another gulp.

"Nico, what did ADFD stand for again?"

"Well, they stood for an end to war, coloured shirts and a love for all creatures."

Thomas rolled his eyes and sighed, "No, you idiot, what did the name mean?"

"Oh, Apples Don't Fall Down. Apparently, it was because the lead singer's grandmother was called Granny Smith and the lead singer's child was called Apple," explained Nico.

"Yeah, yeah, but it's still a strange name," said Thomas.

Nico nodded in agreement, "Yes, that it is, that it is."

The King got up to get another beer, "So, they have a concert on then?" he asked.

"Yes, and well I know it's a bit late notice Thomas, but they're playing tonight and I thought you might like to go?"

"Yeah Nico, that'd be great! What time?"

"I already said, it's tonight," replied Nico, rather confused.

"No, what exact time tonight?" asked Thomas, as he handed his friend another beer.

"Oh yes, 8 pm precisely."

"Right Nico, I'll be there."

The two men continued relaxing and drinking until it was teatime at the castle and Thomas invited Nico to a royal beans on toast. The King thought it unwise for his friend to go to a Bed and Breakfast and ordered that they attend the concert together and then return to the castle, where Nico could sleep it all off in the west wing.

Chapter Three
The Big Bash

Upon arrival at the rock concert, the two men were both surprised and dismayed to find so few people their own age there. Everyone was a good deal older than they were.

"Over 65's get in free," chortled a merry old man as he passed by.

"Oh well, at least we'll out dance them," said Thomas.

On a particular song the art of head-banging was called for. Thomas and Nico felt that they could best demonstrate this to the older generation and so launched forward into full head-banging fervour and managed to bash each other, not once, but twice. The second bash was just too much for them and, as the motionless pensioners looked on, the King and his friend slid into unconsciousness.

They awoke to find themselves at Nadi's house. The police had left and their wives were now taking care of them. The men could not remember anything. Not the concert, nor their wives, nor their children, nor even who they were. Upon realisation of this fact, the women were presented with a myriad of options and opportunities. Nadi pulled Esmerelda aside and said, "Sweetie, this is what you've always wanted. You can de-throne the King and become ruler yourself. You can change all the laws that restrict us."

"Don't be silly," whispered Esmerelda, "I don't want that. I don't want to leave my husband or be ruler in his place or change any laws, even those that are restrictive. All I want is my husband back."

"Yes, ok, but what about a new and improved husband, a better ruler and a better man?"

"What are you saying Nadi?"

"He's a blank slate, Es. He doesn't even know who he is. You can show him. Do you understand me? You can help him to be the husband he always could have been, the one you always wanted him to be?"

Esmerelda seemed troubled; "Oh I don't know. It doesn't seem right somehow."

"Well, would you like **me** to help him?" suggested Nadi.

"No, that won't be necessary," replied the Queen, firmly, "but I'm not gonna lie."

"You don't have to, Es. All you have to do is help him to improve. Besides, you will have to explain to him what he does for a job, not just who he is as a person."

Esmerelda looked very worried, "That's true. What a daunting task and what about the kids, Nadi?"

"You have a nanny, just pay her overtime for a while and explain to the children that daddy's a little sick at the moment." Nadi placed a reassuring arm around her friend, "Don't worry Es, it'll all work out ok."

The ladies walked over to their husbands.

"Who are you?" asked Thomas, as he gazed at his beautiful wife.

"My name is Esmerelda."

"That's a nice name. Do you live nearby? You're a nurse right?"

"No, I am a queen."

"Wow, a queen! What an honour. Why do you come to me then? Am I important?"

"No, not really, you are just a king."

"Oh wow! From a different kingdom?"

"No, same Kingdom, different place."

The King leant forward, quite intrigued, "So what place am I from?"

"Mars," replied Esmerelda.

"What place are you from?"

"Venice."

Thomas flopped back onto his bed, "Sounds nice."

Nadi called over, "Give him the book to read."

"Oh he won't read that," replied Esmerelda, as she tried to hand back the book.

"Yes, he will now," insisted her friend.

The King snatched the book out of his wife's hands and read the title aloud. "'Men Are From Mars. Women

Are From Venice.' Is it a Science Fiction novel? I think I remember liking those."

"Er, not exactly," replied Esmerelda nervously, "it's a relationship guide."

"Do I like those?"

Nadi interrupted, "Yes, you love them, you read them all the time. The only thing you like more than them is romantic musicals and clothes shopping trips with your wife."

"Really?" asked Thomas, rather surprised.

Esmerelda walked over to her friend, "Nadi, what are you doing?" she whispered. "You know he hates those things."

"Not anymore he doesn't. Oh no, not anymore," said Nadi, as she smiled and thought about what delights her husband would now be into himself. She thought of him finally doing work around the house, looking after the kids, taking her on romantic days out and waving credit cards in front of her, enticingly. Oh yes, life was gonna be good in their household from now on.

After months of being everything their wives could ever want in a husband, two worn out men and two dissatisfied women met at opposite ends of the Kingdom, to talk and reflect.

"Want a beer?" asked Thomas.

"No, only drink herbal tea," replied Nico.

"I somehow don't think that's true, Nico. I don't remember much, but I remember a few things. I remember loving sleep and beer. I just don't remember ever liking shopping, books and musicals."

"Yes, I know what you mean Thomas. I never remember staying at home and looking after the children, but I do remember..."

Thomas turned to him, "What?"

"I don't know," sighed Nico, "I forgot."

The King got up to get a drink for his friend, "At least have a beer, man."

"No thanks Thomas, my wife said if I drink it I'll grow a third nostril."

"That's rubbish, Nico. I tell you what, you drink it and I'll hold your nose to stop it sprouting a third nostril."

"Well ok, sounds reasonable," replied Nico as he grabbed the beer from Thomas and took a gulp, "Jolly nice stuff this is. I think I'll drink the lot."

"What are you known as Nico?"

"Nico the Nice is what I go by."

The King spat out a mouthful of beer in disgust, "That's horrible! I think you should be re-named. Got any ideas?"

"Well, I've always quite liked Nico the Excitable as a name for myself. Even though I don't have much excitement these days, I do long for it. My wife tells me that I've never really been into all that going out and having exciting times, but I don't know, in fact, I'm not sure."

"Yes, definitely something fishy going on here, anyways, another beer Nico?"

"Yes I think I will, Thomas. Thank you very much."

Meanwhile, a very different conversation was going on at Nadi's place.

"So, you're actually teaching him to knit, Es?" giggled Nadi.

"Yes, I told him that he'd just forgotten how to do it, that's all," smiled the Queen.

"Yes, that's what I tell Nico. He never questions the information, but..."

Esmerelda leant forward in her chair, "But?"

"He's well behaved, courteous, useful and kind, but he's not my husband. I thought he'd still be my husband, only slightly improved, but he's someone else. Someone I've invented and so," Nadi paused to wipe a tear from her eye, "I'm not happy being married to a robot, Es."

"Yes, I know what you mean," sighed Esmerelda as she handed Nadi a tissue, "Thomas isn't my Thomas, as he used to be. I'd rather have an imperfect husband, who was hardly ever around, than a perfect one who was so perfect that he irritated the living daylights out of me. The last law he passed banned men from leaving the house. Now we have unemployment problems across the kingdom, as half the workforce is house-bound."

A tear fell from Nadi's face, "Yes Esmerelda; we definitely need our old husbands back, warts an' all."

The Queen took her friend's hand, "Yes and they need their less than perfect wives to help them remember."

Nadi suddenly looked worried, "Es, your husband will have our heads for this! What we did to him could be seen as treason."

"No, we'll be ok Nadi, because we're not gonna tell them."

Nadi was shocked, "We're not?"

"No, we're gonna hit them."

The Queen's suggestion just confused poor Nadi even more, "How will hitting them help, Es? I mean, after all, that's what got us into this whole big mess in the first place."

"Exactly Nadi and hopefully that's what'll get us out of it too."

Nadi looked unconvinced, "Oh dear, my Queen and friend, I hope you're right, I really do."

The female pair hatched their cunning rescue plan and the male pair slowly recovered their memories, as the sun began to go down and night cast itself over the Kingdom. The final showdown would have to wait until morning now. Would the men have fully regained their memories before their wives reached the castle? Or would the women be able to bash them back to the end of the rock concert?

Chapter Four
Rescue Plans

Morning arrived rather speedily for the women, who bounced out of bed and collided with each other on the way to the bathroom. When they regained consciousness neither one of them knew where or who they were. Thankfully, this passed after about five minutes and they breathed a sigh of relief. All they needed now was for them to be in the same state as their husbands had been.

"If I had not regained my memory I wonder if Thomas would have tried to do to me as I did to him?" thought the Queen aloud.

Nadi looked at her friend and laughed, "Well, you certainly would have deserved it."

Esmerelda frowned at her.

"I mean, **we** certainly would have deserved it," added Nadi wisely.

"That's better. After all, you weren't exactly the mother of all morals were you?"

Nadi looked down in shame; "I suppose not Es, no."

"Well Nadi, we can't just sit here chatting all day. We have urgent work to do," said the Queen as she 'rose to her feet.

"You are so right my dear. You can have the bathroom first, as you are the Queen. Meanwhile, I will look for something heavy to hit our husbands with."

"Yes alright, but Nadi try to pick something that won't kill them."

With that final piece of advice firmly between her ears, Nadi got up from the floor, walked out into her garden shed and browsed. After a little while her eyes rested upon a mallet, "No, way too dangerous. It's no use; I can't find anything here. I'll just have to bash their heads together, that's all."

Nadi marched back into the house and found Esmerelda towel drying her locks, so decided she would just nip into the bathroom for a moment or two herself.

Quite some time later, Nadi was distracted from her preening by loud knocks on the bathroom door.

"Come on Nadi, you've been in there for ages. How long are you gonna be? As your Queen, I demand that you exit the bathroom, immediately."

"What do you say as my friend then?"

"The same jolly thing, silly," snapped Esmerelda. "Now come on or we'll be using torches to find the men."

Suddenly, the catch clicked back and the bathroom door flung open to reveal a mostly manicured, partly painted and completely cleaned, Nadi; "Alright, I'm done, Miss Impatience," she moaned.

"I hardly think I'm impatient Nadi. You took longer than my entire household to get ready. Anyway, we must leave now, and you don't need that."

Nadi dropped the vanity bag and stopped filing her nails, as the two women exited the tent and entered the Forest of Excitement.

As they strolled along the forest path the Queen could not help but admire the places people had built. She turned to her friend, "Nice villas around here Nadi. So why do you and Nico live in a tent?"

"He likes the outdoors, Es."

"Oh," smiled the Queen.

Once the ladies reached the Glade of Gladness, they stopped for a mug of coffee at Nadi's favourite café, The Mad Mugger. Esmerelda was far from impressed, "I don't know why you like this place Nadi, it's so uncouth."

"Yes," replied Nadi, dreamily, as she was soothed with another sip of her drink, "but the coffee is out of this world."

"So are the people," said the Queen.

After Esmerelda left a tip for the waitress, something like: 'be quicker next time and make sure the coffee's hot', they re-embarked upon their journey.

Meanwhile, back at the Castle, the King and Nico were pacing the floor. They were trying to work out if anything, of what their loving wives told them, was true.

"My wife's no liar," said Nico.

"No, I don't doubt you," replied Thomas. "Therefore, it all must be true. You must really like staying at home."

"No, I love the outdoors life. That's why I live in a tent."

"Then your wife must have lied to you, Nico."

"And yours to you, Thomas."

"Yes, but why?" asked Thomas. "Why say to me that I liked knitting or enjoyed taking her for days out? I can't think of anything I like less than poncing around shops and going on double dates."

"Yes, that's definitely not like you," agreed Nico.

The King jumped to his feet and started to head towards the door, "Right Nico, I tell you what we're gonna do. We're gonna go to your house and have a little talk with our wives, straighten all this out. After eighteen years of marriage, I should know all there is to know about straightening things out. I should be the chief straightener by now."

"Here, here," said Nico, as he followed his friend and master out of the door.

As the women neared the castle, they spotted their husbands in the distance.

"Quick hide!" screamed Nadi, as she grabbed Esmerelda's arm and pulled her behind a nearby blueberry bush.

"Ouch, Nadi, you brute," said the Queen as she rubbed her sore arm.

"Sorry, it's just that I'm not ready to see them yet."

"Well, Nadi, you're gonna have to see them sooner or later."

A little time passed before the women could hear the familiar voices of their husbands. Suddenly, as the men neared the bush the women were hiding behind, they stopped, well, at least Nico did.

"Look Thomas, blueberries!"

The King sighed, "I hardly think this is the time to go blueberry picking, Nico."

"Any and every time is the time to go blueberry picking, old chum," replied, the ever positive, Nico.

"Well, for goodness sakes, hurry up then!" growled the King.

"Yes, yes, yessity yes," said Nico, as he frantically picked away at the blueberry bush. The women tried to stay as still as possible and desperately control their breathing. By the time he'd stripped the bush almost completely of its fruit, a thought suddenly dawned on Nico, "I've got nothing to put these in."

"You idiot Nico! In all your excitement, you didn't even think of what you would do after the immediate situation in front of you."

"Neither did you."

As the two men argued, the ladies could hold it in no longer and burst out laughing.

"Did you hear that?" asked Nico. "It sounded ever so familiar to me. I hear that same sound every time I try to spell a long word in Scrabbled and there's only one person I ever play Scrabbled with."

Thomas rolled his eyes, "Gosh Mr Observant, like we don't already know it's your wife in there."

"Where?" asked Nico, his head turning this way and that.

"The bush, you idiot. It's alright ladies, you can come out now."

Out they came; they skulked along like naughty children, just exposed by disapproving parents.

"I think it's time we all sat down and had a little chat, don't you?" said Thomas.

The women nervously agreed. The little chat was indeed just that, little. After about five minutes the talks broke down and screaming and shouting ensued. However, once Nico calmed down, it was plain to see that the men still felt very betrayed and the women guilty and extremely nervous. Was this the end of their marriages? Had they gone past the point of no return? Esmerelda had one last plan she hoped, beyond hope, would save them all. The plan's name was Mrs Iva Mary Husband--Marriage counsellor extraordinaire and close friend of the Queen's cousin, so available at a special rate (except on weekends and during the week between 9 am and 5 pm; subject to terms and conditions etc etc.)

"No way!" said the King, when he heard of his wife's marriage counsellor plans.

"Oh come on Thomas. Nico and I are gonna do it," said Nadi.

"Are we?" cried a rather surprised and alarmed Nico.

"Yes we are dear," replied Nadi, through gritted teeth.

Suddenly a new and unfamiliar voice spoke up, "If I may be so bold as to suggest something radical and completely amazing?"

The King looked around to see who had spoken.

"I'm down here."

After the King had looked everywhere in a desperate attempt to follow the sound of the voice, he finally gazed intently at the ground to discover a snail had spoken.

"I never knew snails could speak," said the King.

"Well, yes we can, but I have to make sure I stick my head out of the shell or I get an echo."

"Must be quite a lot of room in there, I'd expect?"

The snail was quite offended by the King's last comment, "Are you saying I'm fat?" he blasted.

"No need to get shell-shocked," replied Thomas.

The snail rolled his eyes, "Do you really know how many times I've heard comments like that?"

"No, not really."

"Hardly ever, because it takes someone of extreme stupidity and utter brainlessness to come up with them. Rather like yourself, actually."

"Don't forget I can tread on you," threatened Thomas, as he dangled his foot over the snail.

The snail gulped and Esmerelda interrupted this show of kingly strength, "You just dare, Thomas. I think he's rather sweet. What's your name?"

"Samuel, but you can call me Sammy."

"Sammy the snail, that's cute," laughed the Queen and then asked, "So, what was it you were going to tell us that was so radical and amazing?"

"Oh yes, my wife had some difficulties in our relationship and we went to visit Mrs Iva Mary Husband. I didn't want to go at first, but was tempted into it by the offer of free food and drink and I've never looked back since. She's the best around and certainly saved my marriage."

"Did you say something about free food?" asked Thomas.

"Yes, and lots of it too."

The King's face brightened like the sun, "Well then, what are we waiting for? Book us up."

Esmerelda seized her chance and ran at top speed to the nearest phone, before her husband changed his mind.

Both ladies slept well that night in the knowledge that their problems may all be over soon.

Chapter Five
Iva Mary Husband

The day of the marriage counsellor appointment dawned brightly. An excited Queen leapt out of bed and drew back the curtains of the Royal bedchamber. "Wakey! Wakey! Dear," she chirped.

Thomas gave a massive yawn, "What time is it, Esmerelda?"

"Time for you to get ready to eat like a horse, I guess."

With those words still ringing in his ears the king did a rather energetic leap to the bathroom.

Ready ten minutes later they set off for their session with Mrs Iva Mary Husband. After a while on the journey the King began to grumble, "Cor dear, how much further is it? I didn't even know I owned this much land!"

"Stop moaning Thomas, we're almost there," snapped Esmerelda.

Finally, Thomas and his wife arrived in the vicinity of The Clinic for Marital Happiness. As they drew near, the

Queen thought she spotted their good friends Nico and Nadi. She pointed this out to her husband. His reply was scornful, "Listen dear, that can't possibly be them, that couple look like little love birds, all of a twitter. Look at them giggling and blushing, and that's just the man. There should be a ban against that sort of thing. In fact, I think I'll ban it as soon as I get home."

The Queen waved at what she thought to be Nadi.

"Oh great," groaned Thomas, "now look what you've done Esmerelda, they're coming over."

Sure enough, the merry couple soon met up with Thomas and his wife. The man turned to the King, "Howdy doody Thomas, old pally?" he asked.

Thomas was completely stunned, "Sorry, but for a moment I thought you were addressing me, but then I don't know anyone stupid enough to address me like that."

The man just laughed and gave his wife a kiss. By now it was obvious to Thomas and Esmerelda that this couple were their friends, Nico and Nadi. Though, why they were behaving in such an odd manner was extremely puzzling.

"My husband is simply adorable, isn't he?" giggled Nadi, like a little girl.

Esmerelda could not believe what her friend had just said, "Nadi, are you drunk?"

"Only on love my dear, only on the sweet love of my husband. My little Nico-Nico poop."

"Don't you mean Nico-Nincompoop?" asked Thomas. "I shall never play golf with him again. I can imagine him at the game asking for a club, 'Oh just give me any of the shiny ones to hit the ball with.'"

"Well, I happen to like him like this," snapped Nadi.

"Come on Thomas," motioned Esmerelda, "let's at least go in and try to work out what they did to our friends."

"Yes, most definitely," agreed Thomas. "I intend to get to the bottom of this. I knew I should have trod on that snail while I had the chance."

As they entered the clinic Mrs Iva Mary Husband's secretary met them. The Queen spoke first, "Iva Mary Husband?"

"Yes, haven't we all deary?"

"No, what my wife means is that we have an appointment with her now," interjected Thomas.

"You can't possibly have an appointment with her now my dear because she is with someone else at the moment, but if you both cuddle over there on those heart shaped cushions she will be with you shortly, I'm sure."

Thomas leant forward, his face crimson with anger, "Now listen here my good lady. I am King Thomas and as such demand an appointment immediately, this instant, now, in a moment or none!"

The secretary raised her eyebrows, "Well I can see why you're in here, but you being King will not change anything. Even if I were to be beheaded for denying you access I would still be required to sit here in headless position and block your way."

Thomas calmed down; "I'm not going to behead you. I wouldn't waste a perfectly good axe on your proud little neck, deary," he said spitefully.

"Well, I must say," gasped the secretary, "the sooner you go in there the better, if you ask me. That temper of yours is the first thing you should try to lose."

The secretary turned to Esmerelda, "I don't know how you do it love," she said. The Queen gave a half smile and proceeded to sit on a love cushion next to her sulking husband.

After waiting several minutes longer than you might for a dentist or a doctor, it was finally time to enter Mrs Iva Mary Husband's lair. Thomas and Esmerelda sat down to face Iva. She was about five feet, five inches in height, of portly figure, with short black hair and a long nose, surrounded by chubby, yet rosy, cheeks.

"Hello my dears," said Iva. "Where on the great path of marriage do you wish to venture today?"

"What on earth is she talking about?" asked, a rather bewildered, Thomas.

Iva's beady eye caught the King, "Ah, the man in denial yet again. I take it you came for the food?"

"Yeah," snapped Thomas, "and an explanation."

"Well, it's about two people who leave their separate lives and their parents and are joined together through..."

The King interrupted, "No, not an explanation of marriage. I wanna know what on Habblespacks River you did to our friends?"

"You have friends? I find that quite amusing," laughed Iva.

"Well, we did have until you finished with them," said Thomas, "we just met them outside and they are by no means the same couple we knew yesterday."

"Well, of course they're not," smiled Iva, "we don't mess around in here you know. Our rates may be reduced, but our services are not, that's for sure."

"Look, just tell me what happened to them," said the King.

"Well, let me see now. There was a lot of crying, a bit of hugging, the occasional slap and then the usual apologies etc etc."

"That sounds like a typical Sunday afternoon at their place. Are you sure there wasn't anything else?" asked Thomas.

"No." Iva thought for a moment. "I mean we always give each couple a rather large bottle of complimentary champagne."

"Well, why didn't you say so before? That's what happened. I bet you they drank the whole jolly lot. What I'm wondering though is whether they drank it to cheer themselves up and try to forget your miserable session? Or did they feel so happy with your help that they celebrated and over-indulged themselves?"

"Oh, obviously the latter. I've never ever had a complaint from any of my clients," replied Iva, proudly.

"Yet," muttered the King.

"Oh Thomas! Give her a chance will you? You always judge people too quickly."

"Does he Esmerelda dear?"

"Yes, he's a jolly rotter sometimes."

"Does he judge you often, my dear?"

"Well, actually no, hardly at all really." Esmerelda hung her head in sadness; "He'd have to be around more to do that."

Iva Mary Husband turned to the King, "How do you feel Thomas?" she asked.

"Hungry Iva. I could eat a horse."

Iva pushed the intercom button on her desk and ordered the food and drink to be brought in, then asked; "Now how do you feel, Thomas?"

"Ah yeah, this is good," said the King, as he munched away on a leg of lamb. "I feel much better now, thanks."

"But how do you feel about what your wife just said?"

"Did she say something? I wasn't really listening, to be honest."

"She said that you don't judge her because you're hardly ever around."

The King had a mouth full of lamb, which showered everywhere, as he replied, "Yes, it is true that if I was around more often I'd probably be able to judge her more."

"But she doesn't want to be judged. She's not asking for that, but more of you being around."

"I am around. In an around-about kinda way."

"What does that mean exactly, Thomas?"

"I dunno, just a play on words."

Iva leant forward in her chair and Thomas could smell her egg salad breath, in fact, he could even see some vague strands of salad trying to make their escape through her front teeth. Suddenly, his egg salad thoughts were interrupted by the most peculiar of questions from Iva; "Do you love her, Thomas?"

"Erm, what's love got to do with egg salad?"

"I beg your pardon?" replied, a rather shocked, Iva.

"You have egg salad stuck in between your front two teeth."

Esmerelda held her head in her hands and gave a deep sigh.

"Oh, how clever of you to notice," said Iva, "but I have a feeling you were trying to avoid the question I just asked of you."

"What question?"

"Ah denial. You know, the question," said Iva, as she tried to pick the strands of salad from her teeth.

"Come on, give us a clue?" moaned Thomas.

"Erm, you know, about whether you...oh fiddlesticks, now I've forgotten the question."

There was one deeply frustrated person who would never allow herself to forget the question. She sat up in her chair and turned to her husband; "Iva asked the question, 'Do you love Esmerelda?' I need to know the answer, Thomas."

Thomas gulped, not just once, but twice. Why on earth was his heart beating faster? He hadn't just done any strenuous exercise. What was wrong? Thomas started to go red. Beads of sweat swam down his face. Here he was the King of all this land and yet a right mess and shiver over one simple little question. Well, it was no good sitting there all day. As a King he must, at times, do the bravest of deeds. Thomas turned to look at his wife. He felt particularly drawn to her eyes. After all these years, had he not noticed how beautiful they were? How slender her nose? How rosy her cheeks? Wait a minute, that wasn't his wife; it was the marriage counsellor.

"Right, I'll turn the correct way this time," thought Thomas. As he did so, he saw nothing but empty space.

"You'd better run after her. She saw you staring at me," warned Iva, as she checked herself out in a nearby mirror.

Thomas lost no time at all as he raced outside to find his wife. He spotted her sitting under a big oak tree, chatting to some old man with a frothy white beard.

"Get away from my wife, you old codger," barked the King.

The old man, not wishing to cause a scene, exited without a whisper of commotion.

"He was too old for me anyway," laughed Esmerelda.

Thomas sat down next to her. He briefly remembered how excited she had been about today, "I'm sorry if I ruined your day."

"It wasn't just **my** day Thomas. It was meant to be **our** day. I left the clinic because you couldn't even answer a simple question. I realise ours was an arranged marriage; I could expect nothing less as a princess, but I was so overjoyed when I found us falling in love. Now eighteen years later you can't even answer that simple question. Thomas please just tell me, yes or no. Do you love me?"

There was a pause as Thomas began to realise what his wife was asking. This was no simple question. This time his eyes met hers and locked. Wow, and he thought the marriage counsellor was beautiful! He saw both a depth and a sorrow in Esmerelda's eyes. He wondered why he had not taken the time to study his wife more closely. How could he have missed all of this? Yes it was true he had loved her, but now things were different. Now, at this precise moment, he was beginning to fall in love with her.

"Yes."

Esmerelda kept staring back into his eyes. "I don't want to blink in case I miss anything. Tell me again."

"Yes, Esmerelda, I do love you. I can't prove it right now, but I'm actually falling in love with you as we speak."

"Wow, how is that possible Thomas?"

"I'm sorry, but I think it's because I've never stopped to get this close to you."

A tear swept the face of the King.

"Are you crying Thomas?" asked Esmerelda, gently.

"No, my eyes are watering because I'm staring at you without blinking."

The Queen smiled, "Then you'd better blink, we wouldn't want you to be crying."

Thomas blinked and then asked a rather awkward question, "Did you see me eyeing up the marriage counsellor?"

"No, but why would you do that? She's about seventy-five."

"So, you're not jealous then?"

As those words rang in her ears Esmerelda began to laugh, while Thomas breathed a sigh of relief.

It was not too long after they had finished their kiss and cuddle that a newly revived King and Queen re-entered the Clinic. Mrs Iva Mary Husband was very pleased to see them again and put down her coffee and magazine as they strode into her office. The first words that left Iva's mouth were one's of great instruction and wisdom, "I will have to bill you for the time spent outside of my office too, but you can pay in monthly instalments, if you like."

The newly romantic pair didn't seem to notice a word she had said.

"Of course you're still not quite finished, but I can see you've come a long way. It would be foolish of me to ask if the question was answered. It obviously was. So onto our last section, if you can stop canoodling and kissing long enough?" said Iva.

Thomas had never applied his, 'I'm King and I'll do as I like,' policy to kissing his wife before, but now seemed as good a time as any. However, he did keep one ear on the teachings of Iva. Esmerelda managed to keep both her ears on the teachings because she was able to multi-task.

"Love is not a feeling, though feelings can go with it. Love is about those decisions you make each moment of the day, both big and small. Love is about you being unselfish and thinking of your spouse first."

Suddenly Thomas stopped kissing his wife, "Eh? But I'm King!"

"Yes, but if you want a marriage fit for a king you must exercise a bit of give and take," warned Iva.

"I'm good at the take part already and I'm sure I can teach my wife to give."

"Wait a minute Thomas, haven't I given you enough already?"

"Woah there you two! Before you lock antlers, I would like to help you practise what I preach. All you have to do, to start off with, is find one thing a week to do for your partner that is not about you, but them."

"Ooh, sounds a bit tricky to me."

"Oh come on Thomas. It's only one thing a week," said Esmerelda as she turned to him and looked deeply into his eyes.

"How's she doing that? She's changing my opinion with a look. Now I know why I wasn't around as much. Oh I can't help it." Thomas agreed to sign up to this plan of action and wondered what terrible things he might have to suffer for his wife. He knew that a shopping trip could have an inconceivably bad effect on him--let alone her music and movie collection, which was the complete opposite of his. No such thoughts were in the mind of Esmerelda, she was too busy worrying about whether this was all a dream and if anything had really changed at all.

Chapter Six
The Turnaround

A few days later the King walked into the kitchen and caught sight of two tickets on the table. He noticed they were for a rock concert. Not just any rock concert, but for one of his favourite bands, "I don't remember buying these," he thought aloud.

"You didn't."

"Oh you're in, I thought I was alone in the house, Esmerelda."

"I bought those tickets," said the Queen.

"You?"

"Yes Thomas, me."

"Are they for Nico and I?"

"No, they're for us, honey."

Thomas was amazed, "But sweetheart, you hate rock, particularly the kinda rock these people play."

"Yes I do, but I thought it would be a good way to put what we learned at the clinic into practise."

"Are you sure you wanna go?" asked Thomas in surprise. "I mean it's really loud, obnoxious and sometimes downright egotistically scary."

"I'm used to that," smiled the Queen.

"Well, alright then," said Thomas, as he hugged Esmerelda with joy.

Little did they know that almost exactly the same situation had played out, just a day earlier, at Nico and Nadi's place. Nadi had even brought tickets not too far from the same patch of ground as Esmerelda.

"Hotdogs are so expensive these days," moaned Thomas, as he and Esmerelda entered the concert arena. Esmerelda had tried desperately to appear happy with the whole affair, but it was so frustratingly difficult. This was definitely not her scene. Lager flowed like a river, food was as cheap and cheerful as could be and about as healthy as sucking raw eggs.

"Urgh!" screamed Esmerelda, as someone was sick inches from her feet.

The King was in his element, "Isn't this great honey?"

"Yes, quite amazing dear," replied Esmerelda as she tried to avoid walking on any vomit.

To say that the band began to play was perhaps an overstatement. They began what, to the musically educated ear, can only be described as hell on earth at about 8 pm. Esmerelda was so very glad that earmuffs were back in fashion at this concert. Just then, to her delight, the Queen caught sight of her beloved friend and confidant, Nadi. She waved desperately at her. As soon as Nadi saw Esmerelda she ran over. However, she slid on some vomit and her head smashed into the Queen's. They both fell to the ground, unconscious. Nico hadn't even noticed his wife had gone and Thomas was fairly slow on the uptake too. Finally, Nico saw Thomas frantically waving his arms like an oversized bird, too fat to fly. Nico ran over, "I didn't expect to see you here old chap."

"Yes, yes Nico, later with the chit chat. Our wives are in trouble."

"Not dead are they?" asked Nico, suddenly quite worried.

Thomas put a reassuring hand on his friend's shoulder, "No, just unconscious. First thing I did was feel for a pulse. I learnt that from the army, you know when we trained with life sized cardboard cut-outs."

"Oh, I see," replied a rather unsure Nico.

The King, being the King, ordered that every medic in the place report to him at once. The response was, at best, disappointing. For no one turned up.

"Do they even have medics at concerts, Thomas?"

"You know what Nico, I don't believe they do. I don't know what those monks do with their herbs and x-ray machines all day, but they ought to be at Chicken Cramp concerts, helping out emergency cases like this. Remind me to make that a law sometime."

"Righty ho mate," chirped Nico, "but what will we do now?"

"Look, Esmerelda and I took the Royal carriage tonight because we didn't feel like walking, so let's carry them over to that and drive them to the local medical centre."

"Good idea. How much excitement can one Nico take in an evening?"

"Pull yourself together man," ordered Thomas.

Thomas and Nico finally arrived at the area the Royal carriage had been parked, but all they found was an empty space. To their horror, it appeared to have been stolen. They had no choice, but to carry their wives all the way to the local medical centre, which was really just a modern monastery. Nico was the first to complain, "It's not fair, all that dieting my wife does and she still weighs a ton."

"I'm glad she can't hear you Nico," replied Thomas. "My wife's, well, quite a good workout herself.

There was a moment of silence, then the King started to complain again, "Who'd have thought we'd go from a great Chicken Cramp concert to carrying our wives to a monastery?"

"Yeah, I know," sighed Nico, "and I think I'm getting chicken cramps, whatever they are?"

Upon arrival at, The Monastery for Medical Modesty and Quietness of Soul and Shoes, Thomas and Nico were thoroughly checked over for spiritually contaminating diseases...and mud. The head monk, Cecil the Impossibly

Quiet, beckoned them in. The women were laid to rest in a sealed off area next to, 'The Quarry of the Unrighteous and Noisy,' which, coincidentally, is near a very good library.

The monks were forbidden to speak inside the monastery and also in danger of a lightning strike if they ventured outside. The head monk, however, kindly made an exception for these poor wretched sinners in their plight. He explained to Thomas and Nico that their wives would soon regain consciousness and that they were very pretty and it was a pity he was a monk. Thomas and Nico resented being called pretty, but calmed down once they realised the man had been referring to their wives.

Relieved that he had not been struck by lightning for going outside, Cecil the Impossibly Quiet made his way back into the monastery and headed towards the sealed off area. He used the mobile monastery satellite phone to call some local nuns to transfer Esmerelda and Nadi to, 'The Nunnery of Niceness,' where they would be fed wild, yet subdued, berries until they were well enough to leave.

It was not long before Nadi and Esmerelda were ready to return home. However, they did not know who they were. They both assumed they might be called Mary because that's what they heard the Nuns of Niceness regularly call out. They also knew that they were sick of berries, wild or otherwise. Were they married to the two men who were now catering for their every need? Nadi was upset that she wasn't the Queen, but glad she wasn't married to the king. Here was a golden opportunity for Thomas and Nico to get their revenge on the wives who subjected them to a false identity earlier in the story. It was at this point, however, that one could see they had well and truly changed. They did not try to re-programme their wives to be all they could ever have wanted in a spouse, although it was rather tempting. Instead they told the truth, the whole truth and nothing but the truth. So happy were they at their husbands' risky honesty, the wives decided to cut them so much slack they could have covered the castle in it. They were free men...for a while... until they discovered, to their horror, that their wives were simply too unwell to look after the kids, go grocery shopping, wash the dishes, and all the other things they had managed not to think about in previous times.

"Whatever you do Esmerelda, stay unwell for as long as you can," whispered Nadi from the sofa opposite.

"I heard that," said a voice from the kitchen.

The wives sat up and looked at each other, "Oh no Nadi," sighed the Queen, "here we go again!"

The End.

King Thomas the Adventurer in...

See a way

First Chapter
A Strange Discovery

Today was an unusual day for King Thomas; it was his birthday. Nothing unusual about that you might say, and you'd be right. Turning forty had never really bothered the King and he'd always enjoyed Royal celebrations. So, what was wrong? What on earth was the matter? Could it be that finally the King was getting just a bit too old? Maybe if he were young again life would be better? Oh such ridiculous thoughts did whirl around the mind of the King. Thoughts he had never bothered to think before. "Before what?" You may ask. Before the accident yesterday which caused the King to be sitting in bed getting medical attention on his fortieth birthday.

The sun was shining, but King Thomas couldn't go outside. All he could do was lie on the hospital bed and reflect, "How on earth had he walked into a lamppost? Could his eyesight have been so bad that he didn't see it?"

Suddenly, his physician interrupted his thoughts, "I'm afraid I have some bad news for you, sire. You are going to need to start wearing these for a little while." The doctor handed Thomas a pair of thick-rimmed glasses.

"What are they?" exclaimed Thomas in surprise.

"They're a relatively new invention called glasses. Just invented last night, actually," said the physician, rather proudly. "You're the first patient to have them."

Thomas' eyes grew wide with amazement, "Wow! Are they safe?" he gasped.

"Oh yes," answered the physician with total confidence.

Thomas put them on and blinked several times, as his baby blue eyes adjusted. The physician leant forward with tremendous curiosity, "How are they, sire?" he asked.

Thomas looked around the hospital ward with great enthusiasm, "Wow, I can see everything in crystal clearness. My goodness me these are amazing, doc!" He stared at the physician's face; "I can count your every wrinkle."

"Well, they must be good. I hadn't even noticed I had any wrinkles," replied the physician as he searched for a mirror.

"Oh yes, you do have quite a few, but don't worry, doc; I could see wrinkles on a new born baby with these."

"Well, I'm pleased you like them, sire, because they cost ten thousand cows."

"How about I keep the cows and you keep your head," threatened the King, calmly.

The doctor gulped and agreed he would rather not be executed over a pair of specs.

A little while later the King's bruises had healed. He was able to go out from his newly built private hospital and into the blazing hot sunshine. He was wearing his glasses, but nobody seemed to notice. When he got back to the castle his manservant Godfrey met him at the door. At first the servant failed to recognize him, but after Thomas removed his specs Godfrey was more inclined to bow and allow.

Just then, Queen Esmerelda walked in and as she saw her husband in his specs she bit her lip, to keep herself from laughing, "What are those awful silly things on your face, Thomas?"

"I think they're called glasses. They're a new invention to help people see in crystal clarity--and they really work."

"Wow!" replied Esmerelda in amazement. "Isn't technology astonishing in the new hospital you had built? Who knows how many people may benefit from similar devices to yours?"

"Absolutely, and I won't have to destroy all the lampposts in the Kingdom now."

"Well that's good. I was not looking forward to a Kingdom of people tripping over each other in the dark every night," laughed the Queen.

The next morning King Thomas leapt out of bed and--onto his glasses. "Snap!" they went and so did the King's attitude of morning serenity.

"Ahh!! Oh, woe is me! Woe is me!" wailed the King. The commotion awoke his beautiful wife. She sat up in bed and started to rub the sleep from her eyes, "What on earth's the matter, darling?"

"I've broken my glasses. I trod on them. They must have fallen on the floor last night and I leapt out of bed this morning, because of a bad dream, and landed on them."

"Oh sweetheart, maybe they can be repaired?" said Esmerelda, sensitively.

"Oh I doubt it, they were only invented yesterday. How will they know how to repair something they've just invented?"

"I don't know honey, but you should at least try to get them repaired, then you'll know for certain where you stand on the matter."

"I suppose you're right," sniffed the King, as he picked up what remained of the glasses.

"What was the dream about, by the way?" asked Esmerelda.

"Oh I dreamt that I broke my glasses in the bedroom by treading on them," said Thomas as he climbed back into bed.

Esmerelda looked surprised, "Really?"

"Yes, really," replied Thomas in frustration. "That's why I leapt out of bed so quickly this morning to see if they were alright."

"Darling, I'm not laughing in a cruel and unsympathetic way, honestly I'm not," said Esmerelda, as she nestled down for a few more winks of sleep beside her rather unhappy husband.

It did not take very long for King Thomas to arrive at the medical centre. A very attractive nurse informed him that the, Lose That Loose Fat, diet class had already begun, and that his personal physician had now gone on holiday for a fortnight. The King was ever so unwilling to wait two whole weeks before seeing in crystal clarity again. He therefore sent his glasses down to the only available lab for repairs of this kind, aptly named, The Lab for Technological Peculiarities and Phenomena, or LTP and P if using hospital jargon. People were usually sent to this lab after sighting strange things in the woods, talking to their shadows, spotting unidentified flying objects or drinking warm alcoholic beverages. No, it was not an asylum for the insane, just a stopover on the way to one perhaps.

Amazingly, only a few hours had passed before the King received the news that his glasses were fixed and as good as new. Elated by this information, the King kissed the attractive nurse on the cheek and asked if she were pregnant due to the bulge in her tummy. He ducked her intended slap and skipped down to the lab to pick up his specs. Obviously, for security reasons, the lab was sealed off, but they managed to pass the King his glasses between the infrared beams and under the padlocked door. Thomas was delighted to receive his specs; they looked as good as new. He tried them on and realised that the attractive nurse was actually not that attractive after all.

Once outside again the King strolled along. He casually took in the sunshine and revelled in his newfound sight. Okay, so the sun almost blinded him and he wished he'd ordered the lab to make a pair of dark glasses too, but never mind.

As Thomas arrived at the castle, he saw the servant girl hanging up the washing and strolled over to her; "Hello Anika, my dear," he said, cheerfully.

The young girl bowed. The King looked intently at her with his new glasses on. He had always thought she had blue eyes, but actually, they were green. Fancy that. As he stared into her eyes, he saw exactly what she was thinking.

"I am ever so sorry Anika, you are right. You do do all this by yourself and I don't ever thank you or give anyone to assist you."

Anika could not believe it and wondered how it was possible for the King to know exactly what she had thought.

"Oh and by the way," said Thomas, "I do appreciate you. Without you I'd never have any clean underwear and clean underwear is of vital importance to me and my kingdom."

"Thank you, Your Highness," said a rather confused and astonished Anika.

"Don't mention it my dear," replied Thomas as he walked away.

The King had not really noticed his new found ability, nor that he had no such ability before he had put on the newly repaired glasses. Into the castle he went and immediately spotted his daughter Lucy. He walked straight by her and then stopped and called out, "Sorry I ignored you sweetheart. You're right, sometimes I am too busy to say hello." Lucy just stood there with her mouth wide open. She stared at her dad in disbelief, "Since when did he ever know what she was thinking?"

The King walked back out of his castle and into the Rose Garden, where his wife was watering her precious flowers, "Hello darling," said the King as he walked over to Esmerelda and gave her a peck on the cheek, "And no, you don't have to worry about that dear, I think she was just trying to be helpful," said Thomas.

"What? Who?" replied the rather bewildered Queen.

"Agnes, our children's nanny of course. Esmerelda, didn't you just say she had told you that the children needed to be on a tighter leash, but that she couldn't find one tight enough?"

"No, I thought that, but I certainly didn't say it, Thomas."

"How odd? Oh well," shrugged the King as he sat down on the grass.

Esmerelda stopped watering her flowers. She simply could not believe her husband's blasé attitude, "What do you mean, 'Oh well?' Thomas you just read my mind in complete, accurate, detail!"

"I did? You mean to tell me you didn't say anything at all?" asked Thomas in surprise.

"No, I didn't. Look Thomas, you normally struggle over reading restaurant menus, let alone minds. It might be a wise move to have a little look through your glasses myself."

"No way!" snapped Thomas. "They've only just been repaired."

"Just for a second. I'll be extremely careful with them," pleaded Esmerelda as she sat down next to her husband.

The King was firm, "No."

She hung her head in sadness, "Oh well, if you can't trust your own wife..."

"Oh, alright then, but be very, very careful with them," warned Thomas.

"I seem to remember that it was the King and not the Queen who broke them last time."

"Yeah, yeah, ok, ok," sighed the King as he took off the specs and reluctantly handed them to his wife.

Esmerelda took the glasses and put them on, "Thomas, I don't always get my own way and no you're definitely not a push-over."

"What!" exploded the King. "How dare you say such things of me?"

"I didn't Thomas, it was you," said the Queen calmly.

"But Esmerelda, why would I say those things to you?"

"I don't know, but I think these glasses enable the wearer of them to read another person's mind, as long as they are close by them at the time."

"But surely that's impossible!" blasted Thomas in amazement.

"Where did you get them repaired?" asked Esmerelda.

"The new lab at the hospital. Why?"

Curiosity suddenly gripped the Queen. "What was the name of that lab?" she asked.

"It was called LTP and P by the staff at the hospital," replied Thomas, still unsure of where his wife was going with her questioning.

"Oh dear," sighed Esmerelda, "that explains a thing or two."

"Why?" asked Thomas, rather mystified.

"LTP and P stands for Lab for Technological Peculiarities and Phenomena."

Thomas looked confused, "I'm sorry, too many long words."

"Basically, they experiment with all kinds of weird stuff in the attempt to invent something meaningful and useful."

"Do they succeed?"

The Queen whispered teasingly, "Nobody really knows. Their work is **so** top secret."

Thomas began to boil under the collar, "But I am the King, there should be no secrets kept from me."

"Well there obviously are dear," said Esmerelda, rather casually.

The King jumped to his feet in fury, "How dare they! I'll keep the glasses, but then I'll find out exactly what goes on down there and, while I'm at it, if they can make me a pair of dark glasses too."

Second Chapter

King to the rescue

Upon arrival at the hospital, the King used all his kingly authority to, quite literally, barge his way into the lab. What he found there simply astonished him. Men in white coats were rushing around carrying strangely coloured liquids in test tubes and beakers. What he assumed were patients were actually drinking these liquids and becoming a little strangely coloured themselves.

"What's all this then eh?" asked the King, as he tried to sound like the head of the local police force. His voice managed to catch the attention of Mr Morphey the chief lab technician, "Who are you?" he asked.

The King was insulted; "You don't know who I am?"

"No, they don't let us out much," came the reply.

"I am the very man who funds you, apparently. I am King Thomas ruler of this entire Kingdom and payer of your pension fund."

Mr Morphey shuffled uneasily, "Oh Your Majesty, I am sorry."

"Yes, quite. Now what on earth are you doing to these poor people?"

"Oh yes, quite a wonderful experiment really. We're trying to see how many different colours we can make a person without any ill effects," replied a rather over excited Mr Morphey.

Thomas appeared confused, "Why?"

"Oh I don't know. I suppose we have a lot of money, but are often quite short of ideas. I know what people say about little green men, but the only little green men we see around here are the one's who get ill from our concoctions."

"I see," said Thomas, rather unimpressed. "So, let me get this right. I fund you people to make other people different colours, and wait until you get visited by someone from a different planet?"

"Erm, yes, but that's not all we do," replied Mr Morphey.

The King sighed and rolled his eyes, "Oh really?"

"No, we also do repairs for things that others won't repair. As well as inventing new medicines and technologies," said the lab technician, rather proudly.

"Yes, I know you do repairs. You repaired my glasses and now I can read minds with them."

"Oh really, and they didn't do that before?" replied Mr Morphey in astonishment.

"No."

"Oh well, that must be our greatest invention yet. Where are the spectacular specs now?"

"In my pocket. I didn't want to wear them in the sun they have a habit of blinding me momentarily when I stare at it," complained Thomas.

"Oh that's not the glasses my Lord. We've known for a long time that staring at the sun, with or without protection, is very bad for your eyes," explained Mr Morphy.

"Really?" replied a rather surprised Thomas. "Well I can see my funding hasn't been completely wasted then?"

"Oh no, certainly not, sire. May I try your specs on my Lord?"

"I suppose there's no harm in that," said Thomas as he handed over the glasses. "I mean at least if you break them you can fix them again."

"Quite, quite."

The lab technician, Mr Morphey, put the glasses on and stared at the King, "Hey! I'm not an eccentric fool who looks even more foolish in glasses," he cried.

"No my good man, of course not," said Thomas as he tried to calm the scientist down. "That was just my thoughts on the matter, my opinion, if you like. You just read my mind, that's all. It's nothing personal old man."

"Right, well yes, of course."

Mr Morphey handed the glasses back to the King, "They are quite extraordinary. I find it almost hard to believe that we invented them."

"Well, actually my personal physician invented them," corrected Thomas. "You just made a few modifications."

"Indeed, but what fine modifications they are you know," replied Mr Morphey proudly.

The King picked up some other bits and bobs from the lab, compliments of the chief technician, and headed home for supper. He was now feeling the satisfaction of no longer being in the dark about the Lab for Technological Peculiarities and Phenomena.

On his way along the forest path, Thomas decided to sit down for a moment and peruse the items he had acquired from the lab. He had: high power stink bombs, itching powder, momentary blindness spray, 'keep your mouth shut' chewing gum, exploding toothpaste, vomit inducing cake, self-inflating rubber dingy and a solar powered flashlight, "This stuff looks grand, but way too dangerous for the odd practical joke, I think. Could be useful in a war or a prison breakout, I guess."

As he sat there beside the forest path a very worried looking man ran up to him and bowed. He then proceeded to hand him a piece of paper. The King read it aloud, "Your Majesty, I bee an' ruthless an' downright nasty man. I bee ruthless because mee roof blew away, so it did. Anyways, enough about me. I bee Paul Daside an' bee wishin' to upset thee. I knows all's about yee top-secret lab because I bee 'avin people at the top who tell me secrets. I 'ave decided that in order to rain down 'avoc on this 'ere Kingdom an' be very bad to very good people

I need money and lots of it. Therefore, I 'ave kidnapped Mr Morphey, your dear lab technician an' am 'olding 'im to ransom. If yee do not give me a reasonable amount of yee gold before 9 am, let's say, tomorrow morning, I will 'ave no choice but to tickle 'im until he cries and then persecute 'im most hideously. I live in the region of Crumbledownia Disgusticas, number 381 Scavenger Avenue. Do not bring anyone wiv yee. If I spot a single soldier, I will start torture immediately.

Yours Sincerely,

Mr Paul Daside
(Part of Paul Daside Enterprises. Making a good day worse than ever)

PS: Just in case you couldn't care less about a scrawny little scientist. I 'ave yee dog Bruno too. Well yee will let 'im run loose in the forest, won't yee?"

The King could not believe it. His own dog Bruno kidnapped and having to stay in a cell with that weird scientist. He must do something immediately, preferably before supper. Now was the time to be brave. The King looked down at the many objects he had acquired from the lab and thought of their usefulness in a daring rescue mission. Maybe, just maybe, he could use them to save his dog and, if time permitted, the scientist too.

"Well, if I'm gonna do any rescuing I'd better start now," thought Thomas.

He hurried back to his castle to acquire a horse, but told no one of his plans, not that he had any.

The King tried desperately to think of a rescue plan as he travelled along, but soon gave up. He'd never been to the region of Crumbledownia Disgusticas before and was getting lost. Suddenly, to help speed the story along, a short, bald, white haired old man appeared out of nowhere and gave him very clear directions to 381 Scavenger Avenue.

When he arrived in Scavenger Avenue, Thomas found a very inhospitable sight. Rows of broken down houses lined the streets. It did not look inhabited and, if it was, the King could not see how anyone could live in such desperate squalor. Finally, he found number 381 and knocked on the bright yellow door. A note was passed to him through the letterbox. It read, 'Go round the back.' Thomas did so and knocked on the back door. He was passed another note. It read, 'Go 'round the front.' The King reluctantly went around to the front door again and knocked. Another note was passed to him. It read, 'Go 'round the back.' By this time he was fuming. Upon reaching the back door, he was passed another note. This time Thomas did not read the note and the door swung open and knocked him back about three paces. When the King regained some sense of consciousness he picked up the note he had ignored. It read, 'Step three paces back.'

Thomas groaned and looked up to the doorway. In it stood a man with a mass of long ginger hair, a very big moustache and a reasonably large bottle of whisky. The man took a swig of his whisky and asked, "Be yee old Tommy the King be yee?"

"Well, I suppose that's one way of putting it," replied Thomas.

"Come yee in. We bin a waiting for yee, we bin," said the man, as he hustled the king in and looked left and right for any sign of the law.

Thomas sat in what some would describe as a chair, while others would feel more comfortable calling it an L shaped piece of rotten wood, supported by four branches.

"Yee thirsty?" asked the scruffy looking criminal.

Thomas looked at the colour of the beverages on offer and wisely declined.

Paul Daside sat down opposite the King, "Well, we be getting' down ta business yee and mee," he said gruffly. "I 'ave yee scientist an' yee doggie. Yee give mee yee gold, I give yee doggie to yee," he paused, "and if yee want, yee scientist too."

Thomas suddenly remembered that he forgot to remember the gold he was supposed to remember not to forget. He shuffled uneasily and broke the, so-called, chair.

"Yee gold if yee please," insisted Paul Daside.

"I don't have it. Erm, I forgot it. Terribly sorry and all that. Maybe you could still release my dog Bruno?"

Paul Daside was furious, "Yee are foolish indeed to forgeet yee gold. Now yee will join yee doggie in yee prison," he blasted.

"My people will come looking for me once I do not return home and if yee, you, keep me here you will receive no gold from me," threatened the King.

Paul Daside looked at Thomas, a wicked glint in his eye, "Not from yee, but from yee wife, the queenie I weel."

Now Thomas was in a whole heap of trouble. Strangely, the King was allowed to keep his unsearched bag with him as he was led into the same prison cell as his dog Bruno and his lab technician, Mr Morphey. How glad he was to see his dog again. It appeared that Bruno was well fed.

"If he looks well fed sire it's because he's eaten all my food as well," said Mr Morphey, with an air of disdain.

"Yes thank you for feeding him, Mr Morphey."

"You can call me Jim, sire, if you wish? How did you end up in here my Lord; I thought you would have sent some royal guards to rescue your dog?"

The King sighed, "No, that was not permitted me. I had to come alone."

"Would you not have paid the ransom then, sire?"

"Yes I would of, but I forgot to remember not to forget to remember the gold."

"Oh I see," said a rather confused Mr Morphey, "You know, sire, it's a pity you don't have those things you took from the lab when we were together last."

"You mean these things?" said the King as he opened his Royal bag to show Jim Morphey.

"I can't believe they let you through with those," replied Mr Morphey in great surprise. "Better keep them out of sight of the guards, they check up on us regularly."

There was a moment's silence and then Mr Morphey said, "Do you know what, sire? I think we may be able to escape using some of these objects. After all I did invent them so I should be able to work out how they can be applied in a situation like this, now shouldn't I?"

"Yes you should. You should indeed," said the King, as he again enjoyed the slobber of his beloved dog.

All evening, in hushed tones, the King and Mr Morphey discussed the daring escape plan they would initiate in the morning. Once clear on the role each man would take they nestled down for a bit of sleep.

Third Chapter
Plans

Thomas did not know how it could have been morning so soon. Neither could he understand how Mr Morphey was able to work out when morning was in a darkened prison room with no clocks. Jim Morphy was first to speak, "Sire, do you remember what you are to do and what you are to use and when you are to do it and when you are to use it and what end to pull and what end not to pull and whether you have the knack yet of pulling it or whether you should practise pulling it again?"

"Sorry?" replied a rather bewildered Thomas.

"No need to apologise, sire. I was just making last minute checks. It seems obvious to me that you are ready, my Lord."

"Erm, yes, quite ready," replied the King.

Of course Thomas actually felt about as ready as a polar bear in a Hawaiian Hula dancing final, but he was King and it would not do to let on so.

Suddenly, the same man as a little earlier in the story--you know the one who spoke in a strange way and wanted the King's gold. Actually his name was, and still is, Paul Daside. Anyway, he politely knocked, coughed twice and unlocked the door to the room of imprisonment. He would cough a third time though. For as soon as he entered the room of imprisonment a reasonably large object was thrown in his general direction. As soon as it hit the ground, a whiff of the most unimaginable horror filled the room. A smell that can only be compared to manure mixed with rotten eggs and a dash of the most hideous flatulence. So strong was the smell that King Thomas fainted before he could reach the door, as did Mr Morphey, but not so with Paul Daside; "Smells almost as good as me old ma's cooking," he quipped.

So the escape attempt had failed and it would soon be time for the first terrifying torture session. They had to act quickly. Plan B must be put into effect after lunch. Lunch consisted of the cooked breakfast Paul Daside couldn't quite manage. He had kindly thought twice about his friends, shown compassion and pulled it all out of the bin, re-heated it, and served it up again. It was at least food, something they had to have if they were to keep their strength up for the next escape effort.

"How did you find it?" said the King to Mr Morphey as they tried desperately to enjoy the last mouthfuls of their lunch.

"Erm, hmm, yeah, well," Mr Morphey coughed and grabbed a glass of very yellow looking water; "I've tasted better. The bacon was a little tough."

"Tough? It was like boot leather," moaned Thomas. "Anyway Jim, enough about the food. What's plan B?"

"Plan B, my Lord, is the following..."

Mr Morphey leant over and whispered this and that to the King, whose eyebrows lifted and arched in response.

"Well, if you think it will work?" said Thomas.

Mr Morphey looked deadly serious; "It has to, my Lord. It simply has to. I have a young wife and two small children at home. They must be going spare with worry."

"Oh, I'm sorry, I didn't know," said Thomas gently.

"That's alright. At least you did try to rescue me," replied Mr Morphey, as he wiped the rest of his lunch from around his mouth.

Thomas got up from the table, "Well, if truth be known, I came for my dog Bruno. You were just an added bonus."

Mr Morphey's face saddened, "No, I quite understand. You being King an' all. I mean what am I and my family when compared to the Royal St Bernard?"

The King patted him on the shoulder, "Quite right, quite right. I see you have a good grasp of priorities Mr Morphey."

"Would you have really not sent out rescue parties if it had only been me here?" asked Jim Morphey.

"Oh my good man, of course I would have," reassured Thomas. "You are a very important scientist in a lab I fund. I have a duty to protect my investments."

"But not because I'm a fellow human being with a family of my own?" argued Jim.

The King shuffled uneasily, "Well, to be perfectly honest," he sighed, "I had not taken that into account."

"If I may be so bold, my Lord? What you did not take into account was, in my humble opinion, the most important thing of all. No human being, whatever their station in life, is beyond being rescued."

"You know what? I suppose you're right. I, as King, should care as much about the individual as the whole. When, or if, we escape I will see to it that my eyes rest on the good, the bad and the ugly, no matter what their position in life may be."

"Very noble of you, sire, but now to the game in hand. As soon as afternoon beverages are served plan B rolls into action. Are we agreed?"

"Yes we are," replied Thomas.

Plan B had been to give Paul Daside vomit-inducing cake, courtesy of the prisoners. Unfortunately, the plan was unsuccessful, as not only did Paul Daside actually enjoy the cake very much, he thought it not unusual to vomit after eating.

Plan C also failed. This involved exploding toothpaste. Unfortunately, Mr Daside never ever brushed his teeth and so the explosion was a no show.

The King and Mr Morphey were by now running out of ideas. Not only that but the torture session was scheduled for the morning. All seemed lost until, suddenly, the King had a stroke of genius. A plan that seemed too good to be true. Sure it would endanger his new friend's life, but it was worth it to escape from this hole of pestilence.

Surprised at Mr Morphey's absurd bravery; Thomas put the plans for plan D, which he planned would be the plan to save them from making any more plans, into position. Plan D was to escape during their torture sessions. Each man would escape individually and then meet up in Don'remane'ere Street. It was a lavishly extravagant plan, fraught with danger, but it was their best chance of escape.

Torture would involve tickling with a feather (even between the toes), stretching (even to touch their toes) and standing for long periods (on the tip of their toes.)

The torture was to be held, rather stupidly, outside. However, in such a deserted neighbourhood men screaming like little girls would go on completely unnoticed. They knew that it was easier to escape outside in the torture garden than upstairs in the room of imprisonment.

A little while later, there was a polite knock on the door of the room of imprisonment and in entered the most intellectually challenged of all criminals. Mr Paul Daside just stood in the doorway and gave a most sinister grin. A grin that was meant to send shivers down the backs of the bravest of men. The King and Mr Morphey concealed their terror well, and even put hand over mouth to muffle any slight giggles.

"I do see yee a larfin' behind yee handies I do, but yee bee a larfin' on yee other side of yee handies when I bee a through wiv yee, yee bee."

"He's jolly clever to see past our handies wouldn't you say, sire?"

"Indeed Morphey. I fear we may be dealing with a personage of the unstablest of IQ's here," agreed Thomas.

"So, who yee of yee two humane beings be first then?" asked the criminal as he twiddled his bushy moustache in the most menacing of ways.

"As King I note that I have certain responsibilities and duties to consider. Therefore I humbly appoint Mr Morphey to undergo the most inhumane torture known to man."

"Yee friendie bee sufferin' terrible for yee if yee don't mindie?" warned Paul Daside.

"How very kind of you to be so concerned about my feelings in the matter of your hideous torture of my friend, but I suppose his sacrifice is truly noble."

"Yee can come down an' watch yee friendie sufferin', if yee likes."

"Your kindness is truly boundless," replied Thomas in an attempt to appease Mr Daside.

"I 'ave bin known for mee kindness sometimes, especially when I bee a sleepin' of a night," boasted Paul Daside.

"Indeed, well it doesn't surprise me really." Thomas made a motion towards the door. "Shall we proceed then?" he asked.

"Yee can 'ave the bestest seat in the garden until it bee your turn if yee likes," declared the criminal, kindly.

"How very kind of you," said Thomas as he and Paul Daside walked out of the door and down the stairs.

All the time the King and Mr Daside had been talking, Mr Morphey had been going over in his mind plan D. He knew that he was not at all ticklish, but was unsure how the King would hold out under such duress. Mr Morphey knew he would have to pretend to be in agony and hoped his village hall amateur dramatics would pass the test.

Fourth Chapter
End in Sight

To cut a long story short, Mr Morphey was indeed tortured by tickling with the lightest of feathers. His screaming was so intense and so dramatic that even Mr Paul Daside could stand it no longer and wished to reach some sort of compromise. Therefore, escape plan D was scrapped. This plan had been to knock out the ten guards, scream and shout, and rush over the eight feet tall barbed wire fence whilst yelling God save the King.

Mr Paul Daside had wondered if there might not be anything else of value, other than gold, on which he could make enough money to fund evil, and thereby let his prisoners go. He turned to Thomas and Mr Morphey and asked, "Have yee anythin' I bee likin' on yee persons. Now don' getta mee wrongly; mee enjoys a wee bit a tee ol' torture now an' agin, but yee screamin' 'an a hollerin' a bit too much for mee weak heart yee see, do yee?"

"Yes, well, I can't think of anything off the top of my head," replied Thomas.

Suddenly, a dramatically weakened Mr Morphey tugged on the King's arm and whispered in his ear, "What about those glasses I fixed for you? Do you have them?"

"Yes, as a matter of fact I do. They've been in my pocket all the time," replied the King in hushed tones.

"Well, they must be worth something, surely?" suggested Mr Morphey.

"Yes Jim, but then he'll be able to read our minds. Not only that, but if he sells them to someone who can replicate the technology I'll have a Kingdom full of mind-readers."

"Better to have a Kingdom full of mind-readers than a Kingdom without a King," replied the scientist, sternly.

Thomas agreed, "I see your point Jim," he sighed. "I'll make the offer."

The King walked over to Paul Daside, produced the glasses from his pocket and said, "We do have these."

The criminal looked rather confused, "What bee them then?" he asked.

"They're called glasses," said Thomas.

"What they do then?" asked a rather puzzled Mr Daside

"You put them on your face. Over your nose and in front of your eyes, then you can read people's minds."

"They bee no good for mee then. I cannie a readie."

"No you don't read minds the same way you read, say, a book," explained Thomas. "You'll be able to read my mind with these on."

"It bee no good to mee if I only can readie yee mindie."

"No, not just my mind, but anyone and everyone's mind."

"Mee try them on, if yee likes mee to?" asked Paul Daside, cautiously.

"Certainly, here you go," replied Thomas as he handed him the glasses and the criminal put them on, with a little help.

Paul Daside blinked several times as his eyes adjusted to the new experience, "Everythin's a lot cleara now," he replied in astonishment.

"Stare at me," said Thomas, as he deliberately thought certain things he knew would mislead the criminal. Mr Paul Daside began to read the King's thoughts aloud, "Yee are right; I bee strongest an' bravest. Yee glasses yee not bee wantin' ta bee partin' wiv because they bee beyond any pricie they bee. I 'ave them I shallest."

"Very good indeed," said Thomas, relieved that Paul Daside appeared to have fallen for his trick.

Suddenly, a most wicked expression spread across the criminal's face; "But yee forgettin'," he warned, "I bee evil an' untrustworthy. I bee sendin' yee back to yee roomie of imprisonment, I bee."

"Oh come on! That's not fair," cried the King.

"I bee evil, not fairie."

As Thomas and Mr Morphey climbed back up the stairs to the room of imprisonment, Mr Morphey leant over and whispered in the ear of the King, "I have an idea that may just get us out of here. It's a long shot, but I'm willing to try anything at this point, my Lord."

"Oi, no whisperin' fom yee," snapped Paul Daside.

Mr Morphey spoke up, "I was just mentioning to the King that we wouldn't want you to do such a terribly wicked and evil thing as to look in the mirror with your glasses on. Gosh if you did that, well, you'd probably know everything about yourself and be so clever you alone could rule the universe or something similar, but slightly smaller in size."

"I bee thinkin' yee be right, I bee."

Once back in the room of imprisonment Thomas spoke, "Jim, why did you tell that madman to look in the mirror? He's sure to do that now."

"Have you ever looked in the mirror with those glasses on, sire?"

"No. With or without glasses on I hardly deem it necessary to be so vain," replied Thomas.

"Quite, well, if you had you would have seen yourself as you truly are."

"What's so bad about that, Jim?"

"You'll see," said Mr Morphey, as he settled his head down on his brick pillow for an afternoon snooze.

It wasn't long after he had left the previous scene that the evil Mr Daside found a mirror in the attic. He blew the dust off and set it against the wall of his room of unacceptable behaviour. He popped the glasses back on and hey presto!...nothing happened.

"I suppose it works better with the light on," he thought as he lit all the candles in the room. Suddenly, all the evil thoughts he had ever thought and all the evil things he had ever done came rushing towards him from the mirror. He could not believe what he was seeing. Could this much wickedness have come from him? He suddenly began to see the results of his evil deeds upon the lives of all the many victims. He realised that the streets in which he now lived were deserted because of him and of his most grievous actions. The experience became too much and he fell to the floor, unconscious.

The thud on the attic floor alerted the guards and cronies, who were of far less IQ than their master. So low was their Intelligence Quota that they each took it in turns to try the experience of gazing into the mirror with the glasses on.

It was not until the following morning that they all finally awoke. The experience had a profound and life-changing effect on them, especially Mr Paul Daside. He now realised in the truest sense that crime doesn't pay. After all, he was still quite poor wasn't he? He could not stop thinking about the unfortunate victims. Some he had made homeless, others he had robbed, and still others he had injured. How was he ever to make amends? Suddenly, his mind flicked back to the King and Mr Morphey still locked away in the room of imprisonment.

His heart sank as he realised that he had kept them from their loved ones for so long. Had he finally become good or was this all just a dream?

A little while later, in the room of imprisonment, our cellmates heard the sound of footsteps.

"That'll be him now, I suspect," said Mr Morphey to the King.

"If it is, then you are much to be congratulated Mr Morphey."

Sure enough, the prison door swung open and there stood Mr Paul Daside. Amazingly, he fell to his knees and begged forgiveness for his cruel torture and imprisonment of them. He most eagerly undid all the chains and allowed them to go free.

The pair, plus Bruno, made their way out of the rundown house and into the equally rundown street. As they walked along, Thomas felt a sudden and unexpected pang of compassion, "I don't feel it right to leave the poor man there. He made his living out of being evil and now that he no longer wishes to pursue that career path, what has he left in life?"

Mr Morphey couldn't believe his ears, "After all he did to us, and you now want to help the man, sire?"

"Look, no man is truly good, but every man is capable of doing good things from time to time. If this man now wants to do good we should help him, regardless of his past misdemeanours," said Thomas.

Mr Morphey was a little hesitant about the King's idea, "How can we be sure he's truly changed?"

The King stopped and looked at his friend, "We can't, but then again life, true life that is, is full of risks is it not?"

"But won't the legal authorities be after him?" argued the scientist.

"I am the legal authority. Look, I'm not stupid. I know he's not a good man, but in that regard how dissimilar is he from me? In my reign, I have thrown people into prison and made families go hungry and been applauded. In fact, it's probably some of my own actions or inactions that have caused this man to enter a life of crime in the first place. No, my good man, we must do the honourable thing. We must invite him over for tea."

"Yes, perhaps you're right, sire. We must learn to forgive and put this matter Daside."

Thomas sighed, "Was that a joke Mr Morphey?"

"Hardly sire, hardly," came the cheery reply.

The End.

About the Author

Hello, my name is King Thomas and I'd like to say a little about the chap who wrote this piece of,erm,...well crafted literature.

He was born in Cambridge, England, but raised in Huntingdon, a small market town, in the same County and, of course, Country.

He has always had a wild imagination and a strange, yet oddly amusing, sense of humour.

Kingly Boredom was written in August 2002 while the author was in Canada. David thought it to be a one off story and three years passed before he attempted to write any more adventures.

August 2005 saw him put pen to paper again and it wasn't long before he had enough stories for his first book.

Printed in the United Kingdom
by Lightning Source UK Ltd.
118510UK00001B/7-87